Taylor, Andrew, 1951-
Blood relation.

$14.95

Blood Relation

By Andrew Taylor

Blood Relation
Toyshop
Blacklist
The Second Midnight
Freelance Death
An Old School Tie
Our Fathers' Lies
Waiting for the End of the World
Caroline Minuscule

ANDREW TAYLOR

Blood Relation

A CRIME CLUB BOOK

DOUBLEDAY

New York   London   Toronto   Sydney   Auckland

A CRIME CLUB BOOK
PUBLISHED BY DOUBLEDAY
a division of Bantam Doubleday Dell Publishing Group, Inc.
666 Fifth Avenue, New York, New York 10103

DOUBLEDAY and the portrayal of a man
with a gun are trademarks of Doubleday,
a division of Bantam Doubleday Dell
Publishing Group, Inc.

Library of Congress Cataloging-in-Publication Data

Taylor, Andrew, 1951–
Blood relation / Andrew Taylor. — 1st ed.
p.   cm.
"A Crime Club Book".
I. Title.
PR6070.A79B56   1991
823'.914—dc20   90-45166
CIP

ISBN 0-385-41761-6
Printed in the United States of America
April 1991
First Edition in the United States of America

10 9 8 7 6 5 4 3 2 1

ONE

IF THERE WERE ANY JUSTICE in this world, the man in the yellow jacket wouldn't have been allowed to live.

The landlady of the Intemperate Frog wanted to kill him. His boots had left a trail of mud across the carpet of the saloon bar. His yellow jacket was exactly the same colour as her aunt's canary. She didn't like the aunt and she didn't like this customer, though not for the same reason.

The man pushed his way into the line of people along the bar. Mrs. Angram delayed serving him for as long as she decently could. While he waited, he leant right across the bar and waved a rolled ten-pound note, held vertically between the first and second fingers of his right hand, to and fro like a pendulum.

Tick-tock, Mrs. Angram thought, tick-bloody-tock. Aloud she said: "Yes?"

"A large whisky. Famous Grouse."

"No Famous Grouse."

"What?" The man sighed. "All right. Bell's."

The yellow jacket was one of those quilted affairs that buttoned up almost to the chin. They had been fashionable a few years earlier, the sort of thing that teenagers bought. The man's hat, on the other hand, was a traditional cloth cap with a beige and black check. Round, steel-rimmed glasses flashed between the collar of the coat and the brim of the cap. Obviously a tourist, Mrs. Angram thought.

It was only September and already the tourists were getting thin on the ground. She could do without this one.

She gave him his glass and he dropped the ten-pound note on the bar, a practice that Mrs. Angram never failed to find insulting. It implied that the customer was afraid of catching a contagious disease from the person serving him.

As she opened the till, she glanced at the clock. It was exactly eight-thirty. The time stuck in her memory because it set off a series of calculations: three hours from now, all the customers would have gone and she could sit down for a cup of tea and a sandwich that she would be too tired to eat; five hours from now, if she were lucky, she would be in bed. She turned round and dropped a handful of change on the counter.

"If you ever come here again," she said, "you'll find a doormat by the door."

"Yes. Have you got a phone?"

"Over there. Just beyond the dartboard."

The man in the yellow jacket was around for perhaps half an hour. Mrs. Angram watched him—not continuously but every now and then; the traffic at the bar was approaching what Jack called its Saturday evening peak, which Mrs. Angram thought of as more like a molehill. First the man went to the phone and made a few short calls—more than one, at any rate; she saw his fingers moving on the dial. In the middle of the first call one of those inexplicable lulls settled over the bar: suddenly almost everyone seemed to stop talking and start drinking. The only sound was the soft thud of a dart hitting the board and the man talking on the telephone.

"Just tell him Oz called, okay? Oz Finwood."

The tide of noise flooded back. Three customers tried simultaneously to attract Mrs. Angram's attention. A little later the man left the phone and demanded another double whisky. Mrs. Angram had recently learned that in the licenced trade you see the human race in simplified terms: people buying drinks, people drinking them, and the drink affecting them. You can separate the casual drinker from the hardened, the solitary from the gregarious, and the gentle from the violent. This man was used to pubs; he drank alone; and—with or without drink—there was nothing gentle about him.

Sometimes the crowd cleared and she glimpsed him standing by the uncurtained window and staring either at the blackness of the night or the reflection of his own face. Inside it was warm but he kept on his coat and cap.

Her husband came into the bar to help with the serving. His cheeks were flushed and that silly RAF moustache of his badly needed a trim. God, he looked a wreck. The last three months had aged him by as many years. And her, for that matter. When dreams come true, there is nothing to stop them from turning into nightmares.

The Angrams carried on a disjointed conversation between customers. These days when they talked, which wasn't often, their conversations were always variations on the same theme. Mrs. Angram slammed the drawer into the till and fired the opening shot.

"You wouldn't believe that carpet was new last week, would you?"

"Bit of mud, that's all. Only superficial. It's a filthy night."

"Superficial? You try Hoovering it then. Have you done the VAT?"

"Don't fuss, Mary. I'll save it till the morning when I'm fresh."

"My feet are killing me. We'll need another barrel of Best soon. It's all villagers tonight, apart from that bloke by the window. And none of them wants bar meals."

"It takes a while for something like this to get established."

"I told you it was a mistake—choosing such a stupid name, I mean. There's nothing worse than a joke that isn't funny. What was wrong with the Crown?"

"There's a million Crowns," Jack Angram said. "There's only one Intemperate Frog. We've been into all that."

"I know. 'It'll attract the carriage trade,' you said. 'The big spenders. The yuppies with weekend cottages. We can build up the hotel and restaurant side.' My God. All you've done is frighten off half the locals."

"It's early days yet." Engines were revving outside. "Hear that? We're going to be busy."

"You know something? I wish we were back in London. With no overdraft and a thirty-five-hour working week. It seems like heaven."

Jack Angram moved away to serve the man with the yellow jacket, who wanted another large whisky. Mrs. Angram scowled at them both. The outside door opened and she forgot her irritation entirely; fear takes precedence over most other emotions.

A group of youths with leather jackets and long, tangled hair shouldered their way across the bar. Each carried a crash helmet. Crash helmets reminded Mrs. Angram of medieval weaponry—one of the less sophisticated varieties, like maces or balls and chains.

"Five pints of Special."

Not exactly carriage trade. They hadn't bothered to close the door. Cold air and menace seeped into the bar. Several of the regulars—and God knew there were few enough of those—started draining drinks and buttoning coats.

The man in the yellow jacket collected his drink and edged away from the teenage bikers. He drank his third whisky more quickly than he had drunk the first two. As he left the pub, he waved goodbye to her.

The wave was so unexpected that Mrs. Angram was too surprised to wave back. She wished she could leave herself, that she were just a visitor here with a nice, cosy holiday cottage waiting for her. No doubt at the end of the week the man had a sensible job to go back to, a decent home in a city with proper shops and perhaps a family.

People with children don't have time for dreams that turn into nightmares. Mrs. Angram envied him.

TWO

ELEANOR LAY BACK and smiled at William Dougal. She writhed and drew up her legs. She was still smiling at him, inviting a response.

Dougal frowned in mock-disapproval. She laughed. It was one of those unbelievably hot September afternoons that fool you into believing that summer isn't really over.

"We'll soon be home," he said. "Your home."

The alteration in her position had made one thing quite clear. Eleanor needed her nappy changed. It wasn't going to be one of those straightforward jobs, either. This one would involve an entire change of clothes. Possibly the pushchair would have to be hosed down with disinfectant.

A lot depended on when it had happened. They had been out for nearly an hour. Dougal knew from experience that a freshly dirty nappy was relatively easy to deal with. The serious problems developed later; and the longer you left them the more serious they became. They sprang from a combination of two factors—the tendency to harden and the tendency to penetrate—and you could never be sure in advance which tendency would get the upper hand. And there were other factors, of course, like diet, mobility and the precise position of the nappy. As with sub-atomic physics, so with children: only the unpredictable was predictable.

Dougal swung the pushchair into Gladstone Gardens with a jolt that made Eleanor gurgle with delight. The road was straight and gave an impression of symmetry. Each side reflected the other: first the Volvos and the BMWs that lined the kerbs; then the lime trees that shaded the pavements and dropped sticky globules on to the roofs of the cars; and lastly the houses themselves, semi-detached late-Victorian villas, each with its own tiny driveway.

The houses must have been designed by a conservatively-minded architect: they were unusually simple for their date. Perhaps it had been cheaper to build them that way. Their depth was far greater than their width. The lack of ornamentation emphasized the box-like simplicity of their shape. On the ground floors the brick had been coated with stucco, moulded to represent dressed stone, and the first floors were faced with grey bricks, which had weathered unevenly to give a dappled effect.

Celia's house was halfway down the road. A beech hedge shielded the front of it from the pavement. Dougal didn't see the Jaguar until he turned into the drive: Celia had a visitor. He was furious because his time here was so precious. He was also a little afraid. It didn't take much to resuscitate the fear that had been with him, on and off, for the last eighteen months. People don't make business calls on Sunday afternoons, even in the public relations industry, or at least not without warning.

The car was black and brand new. Jaguars, Dougal thought, are predators and they tend to be driven by men. Manoeuvring the pushchair between it and the gatepost wasn't easy. He resisted the temptation to see what effect the pushchair would have on the paintwork of the car.

The front door was at the side, set in a pillared porch that deserved to be attached to a house twice the size of Celia's. Dougal rang the bell and strained to hear what was going on inside. Eleanor, perhaps sensing that she no longer had the whole of his attention, began to cry.

The upper half of the door was glazed. Celia took shape on the other side of the stained glass—except she didn't take shape at all; the stained glass and the fact that she was moving towards it turned her into a fluid but abstract mosaic. The porch was out of the sun and Dougal felt cold.

When she opened the door he saw that she was smiling. The smile wasn't directed at him but at the visitor who was somewhere in the house. She looked at Eleanor first, and then glanced up at Dougal.

"You've got a visitor," he said.

"No. You have. It's your boss." The smile broadened and she lowered her voice. "Not at all what I expected."

"You mean he's not a chain-smoker in a dirty raincoat?" Dougal said. "Appearances can be deceptive."

He bent down to lift the pushchair up the steps into the hall. He knew that someone was standing in the doorway of the sitting room, and knew that his words must have been overheard. Eleanor smiled at him through her tears. Sunshine and rain: but where's the rainbow and the pot of gold?

"That's something we all need to remember," James Hanbury said, "especially in our line of work."

Hanbury was wearing a suit of unbleached linen and the Guards tie. The suit was baggy, which helped to conceal the fact that he had recently put on weight. The streaks of grey in the dark hair made you realize how youthful his face was.

"I was just about to make some tea," Celia said. "Indian or China, James?"

James?

"Oh, China please." Hanbury made it sound as if he had been longing for someone to offer him China tea for most of his adult life. "Just as it comes. No milk or lemon."

Dougal lifted Eleanor out of the pushchair. "She needs her nappy changed."

"The bag's in the sitting room," Celia said over her shoulder as she went into the kitchen.

Hanbury stood back to allow Dougal to enter the room first. "Isn't she lovely?" he murmured. "What's her name?"

Eleanor looked unsmilingly at Hanbury and then up at the ceiling.

"Eleanor Rose Prentisse," Dougal said, giving the last word an emphasis he hadn't intended. "What the hell are you doing here?"

"Something's come up."

"I work part-time," Dougal said, "Tuesdays, Wednesdays and Thursdays. Other hours by arrangement. Prior arrangement. And never on Sundays."

"I know. On Sundays you see Eleanor. And Celia, of course. Isn't Celia charming? I can't understand why we haven't met before."

They hadn't met before because Dougal had done his best to make sure that they didn't. He laid Eleanor on the hearthrug and unpacked the nappy bag. Method was crucial in these matters. Spread out the changing mat. Place paper handkerchiefs within easy reach. Select a complete set of fresh clothes. Separate the slimy Baby Wipes from the roll and have them ready for use. Unfold a clean disposable nappy. Find the pot of cream and remove its lid, in case Eleanor's bottom needed soothing.

All this took time. Meanwhile Eleanor herself rolled on to her tummy and waved her arms and legs as if she were investigating the possibility of swimming on dry land. Inch by inch she moved backwards.

"Are you—ah—going to do it here?" Hanbury said, staring at the brown stain on Eleanor's Babygro.

"Yes. Where else?"

Hanbury moved away to the window and looked at the Jaguar instead.

"New car?" Dougal said.

"Eh? Oh yes. I took delivery yesterday. Look, I know this isn't the best of times—"

"After I've changed Eleanor," Dougal said, "I'll get her tea ready. Then she eats it, which isn't a pleasant sight. Then we dandle her on our knees to help her digestion. At half-past six she has her bath. When she's in bed, Celia and I have supper. How did you know I was here?"

"Well, I phoned your flat in Kilburn but there was no answer. I would have phoned you here but Celia's ex-directory. So I thought I'd take a chance and pop down myself."

It really was urgent. It was significant that Hanbury had come himself, rather than despatch a hireling. And it must also be significant, Dougal realized, that Hanbury wanted *him*.

Celia came in with the tea. In Hanbury's honour they had cups and saucers rather than the usual mugs. Hanbury purred with pleasure over his Lapsang. Dougal dropped out of the conversation while he changed Eleanor's nappy; it proved to be a job that needed concentration. Hanbury did most of the talking. He said nothing that was particularly charming or witty—and nothing that Dougal could reasonably take offence at. And yet Celia seemed charmed and amused, and Dougal felt offended.

With the second cup of tea, Hanbury returned to business. This time he chose to do it by a roundabout route.

"I'm terribly sorry to barge in like this," he said to Celia. "You don't mind if I borrow William for an hour or two? I've got a client breathing down my neck. It could be quite a big job—and lucrative, too, for what that's worth."

"It's usually worth quite a lot to William," Celia said. "Anyway, I can't mind lending him to you because he isn't mine to lend."

"A figure of speech," Hanbury said. "Perhaps I should be asking Eleanor."

"Why not discuss it with me?" Dougal said.

"You need the money," Celia said. "Sometimes you've got to put work first. I'll look after Eleanor. If you hurry, you'll be back in time to bath her."

"It shouldn't take long," Hanbury said. "And financially you won't regret it, I can promise you that."

"I've heard that before," Dougal said. "All right. If you both insist."

As they were leaving, he lingered in the hall while Hanbury unlocked the Jaguar.

"There's something I want to talk to you about," he said to Celia.

"About Eleanor?"

"What else is there to talk about?"

. . . .

When they had gone, Celia left the washing up and sat on the sofa with Eleanor. The last of the afternoon sunshine streamed through the big window that overlooked the road.

She found it very difficult to sit there doing nothing; she was out of practice. Eleanor was in a grizzly mood: maybe it was teeth, or maybe she missed her father. Celia hoped it was teeth. The house around her felt huge and empty. Four bedrooms for one person and a baby seemed excessive. The trouble was, Celia decided, she had only been here for three weeks: the house didn't feel like home. Give it time.

The week before she had been interviewed for one of the Sunday colour supplements. They had been doing an article on successful women, which had struck her at the time as one of life's little ironies. The interviewer had been frankly envious of Celia—the house, Eleanor, her job and—above all—the money that went with it. There is nothing like someone telling you how happy you must be to make you realize the flaws in your existence.

Eleanor was sucking the arm of the sofa; a trail of dribble marked her progress. Celia lacked the energy to do anything about it. How on earth had William met James Hanbury? She recognized the type, of course: one of those devious charmers who think they are God's gift to women; there were plenty of them in journalism and public relations.

The washing up was waiting; the unread Sunday papers were a reproach; and, worst of all, Eleanor needed all the stimulation she could get. Instead, Celia wondered whether people ever really changed; what this mysterious job entailed; and what William wanted to say to her. Without Eleanor, of course, life would have been so much easier for both of them. On the other hand, without Eleanor, life would be intolerable.

The phone rang. She lunged for it, nearly knocking Eleanor off the sofa. But it wasn't William.

"Is that Mrs. Prentisse?"

"Actually it's Ms.," Celia said.

"This is Valerie Blackstick."

"Oh good—I was going to phone you this evening. Everything okay for tomorrow?"

"Yes. I just wanted to confirm that there would be no domestic duties whatever. And also the agency should have made it clear that I prefer to go to vegetarian, non-smoking homes."

"Certainly non-smoking," Celia said, "and about ninety-five percent vegetarian. Will that do you?"

"Very well. We'll have to see how the six-week trial goes. I'll be there at two-thirty, as arranged."

"Good," Celia said, suspecting the trial had already begun. "I'll see you then."

She put down the phone. Eleanor grabbed the cord and pulled the handset off the table. Celia managed to prevent Eleanor from toppling after it. Eleanor resented this and started to cry again.

This time, Celia thought, it really sounds serious. What should she do? Suppose Eleanor wasn't just teething or missing William? Suppose she were dying?

"It's a bit delicate," Hanbury said. "That's why I thought of you."

Dougal, who was rolling a cigarette on his lap, said nothing. Silence was often an effective tactic with Hanbury. In this job, "delicate" was a threatening euphemism that could mean "against the law" or even "physically dangerous."

The Jaguar crossed Kew Green and joined the stream of traffic that was inching its way over Kew Bridge. The fine weather had brought people out of their houses and on to the roads.

"The client," Hanbury went on, "requires special consideration. Discretion is even more important than usual. In fact this case may not go through the books."

"That's illegal, isn't it?" Dougal said.

"It's more a matter of bending the rules on humanitarian grounds."

"Why the secrecy?"

"Well—ah—have you ever met Victoria Yarpole?"

"No. I've heard of her, of course."

"The chairman's daughter," Hanbury said. "His only child. Absolutely charming. A free spirit, you might say. Winston is perhaps a mite overprotective with her. After all, I believe she is over thirty."

"So she's got a problem and she doesn't want Daddy to hear about it. Is that it?"

"More or less. Except it isn't really her problem. Though it might be if her father found out about it. You see?"

"No," Dougal said. "I don't."

Hanbury sighed. Dougal stared at Chiswick High Road. Winston Yarpole was more than the chairman of Custodemus: he was also the founder and the majority stockholder. Hanbury had bought into the business last year. Dougal didn't know how much Hanbury's stake amounted to but he carried a lot of clout in the company, and the division he ran had more than doubled in size. Victoria Yarpole was another stock-owning director. Eventually, of course, she would inherit her father's controlling share. Another point was that Hanbury was a widower.

"Winston Yarpole feels his daughter is constantly being pursued by—ah—fortune-hunters." Hanbury hesitated. "Victoria is a healthy young woman—naturally she has boyfriends. At present there is one in particular. She phoned me this afternoon to ask if I would look into him. She'd rather her father doesn't know—I mean, there's no point in upsetting him unnecessarily. Yarpole's a Roman Catholic, quite apart from anything else, and this chap is the next best thing to divorced."

"Before we go any further, I'm not breaking the law. Okay?"

"Of course not. The very idea! But that reminds me: I haven't mentioned remuneration, have I? I was thinking of the overtime rate for the duration of the job. In cash. Plus your normal salary on the appropriate days. How does that sound?"

It sounded illegal, but only just, and also remarkably generous. "It sounds promising," Dougal said.

"You may need a car—you can take one from the pool tomorrow. And I assure you that no one is going to be quibbling about expenses."

"I don't know," Dougal said. "This is such a *delicate* case, isn't it?

And if Yarpole gets to hear about it, my position might be a little delicate too."

"Nonsense. He won't. And even if he did—"

"I do a lot of travelling—for the job, I mean." Dougal thought about those weekly journeys between Kilburn and Kew. "Wouldn't it be cost-effective if you gave me a company car on a permanent basis?"

"Possibly. Oh, all right. For old times' sake."

Hanbury's capitulation was too swift and too complete. It worried Dougal.

"What's the boyfriend been up to?" he said. "Got another woman? Drugs? Or do you just want him vetted?"

"Nothing like that. Or not as far as I know. By the way, you still do freelance editorial work, don't you?"

"A certain amount. I've cut down since I started working for you."

"Have you ever worked for a firm called Gasset and Lode?"

"Once or twice."

"Good. Did you know we do their security?"

Dougal shook his head.

"The boyfriend works there, I gather. In fact he's their publishing director. You might even know him. His name's Oswald Finwood. The problem is, he's disappeared."

THREE

"I CAN'T UNDERSTAND IT." Victoria Yarpole ran her fingers through her long, yellow hair. "It's so out of character. I feel bereft —betrayed. I just don't believe it's happened."

She paced the length of the sitting room and back. Once she stumbled and nearly fell. It was a big room so the walk took some time. Dougal and Hanbury, standing near the fireplace, preserved a respectful silence in the face of such obvious grief. Above the fireplace hung a round, convex mirror in a Second Empire frame. Dougal toyed with the notion that their hostess, who was thinner than most, had bought it to make herself feel fatter.

The exercise seemed to calm her. When she returned to the hearthrug she noticed Dougal, apparently for the first time. She raised her eyebrows and looked down at him. He was a good six inches smaller than she.

"James, who is this?" Her voice was incongruously high-pitched, with the suggestion of a lisp. "I thought you'd be handling the case personally."

"So I shall. William will be assisting me. He's one of my most experienced operatives. And he has inside knowledge of the publishing world."

"You know Oswald?" In just such a manner would Victoria Yarpole's royal namesake have asked if he had known Albert.

"Only by reputation," Dougal lied. "But I've met Josephine

Jones, the editorial director at Gasset and Lode, and a couple of the other editors."

"They're all jealous of him, you know. The Jones woman wanted his job, but they appointed him from outside."

"I can vouch for William's discretion," Hanbury said, "from personal experience."

Yes, Dougal thought, you can do that all right.

"I think I might possibly have a drink. Would you like one?"

She managed to imply that she had magnanimously broken the rule of a lifetime solely for the sake of her guests. Dougal had observed that people who smelled of alcohol often employed this tactic.

"Let me get them," Hanbury said. "You must conserve your strength."

Victoria Yarpole sank on to the sofa in front of the fire. The springs creaked. She might be skinny, but height and heavy bones ensured that she would never be a featherweight. She extended her legs along the sofa and passed a hand with long, red fingernails across her forehead.

"What can I get you?" Hanbury asked.

"Whisky—The Famous Grouse. I keep it for Oswald."

Hanbury and Dougal had the same. While she waited for her drink, she sighed on the sofa—so totally absorbed in her distress that she might have been alone. Only the very rich or the very upset, Dougal thought, can afford to take their emotions so seriously in public. She was wearing what looked like a pair of pyjamas made out of black velvet. Her feet were bare. On her arms were gold bracelets and around her neck a thick gold torque twisted like a hangman's noose. The overall effect, though undeniably eye-catching, was barbaric rather than beautiful: it was as though Boadicea had voyaged forward in time to the late twentieth century and now, stripped of her royal responsibilities, resided in a spacious first-floor flat in Bayswater.

Dougal remained on his feet since no one had told him to sit down. It was Hanbury who eventually waved him to a chair.

"As yet," Hanbury murmured, "William knows nothing beyond

the simple fact that Mr. Finwood has apparently disappeared. Shall I brief him now? You can correct me and amplify as I go."

"Whatever you think best, James. As long as you find him."

Hanbury coughed. "Well, the situation is this. Ms. Yarpole and Mr. Finwood planned to take a week's holiday, beginning today. They were to stay at a country cottage—"

"I *love* the country," Victoria Yarpole said. "I hate London. Oswald is the reverse. He was doing it for me."

"I'm sure he was," Hanbury said. "The cottage is in Powys, just over the border from England."

"Such a curious name: it's called Sheba's Tump, can you believe? I adore these quaint old survivals."

"Yesterday was Winston Yarpole's seventy-fifth birthday. He had a small celebration at home in Wimbledon—just family and one or two close friends. Ms. Yarpole was there. Mr. Finwood wasn't invited—"

"Daddy can be so silly. It will be quite different when he actually *meets* Oswald. You'll see."

"So Mr. Finwood went down to the cottage yesterday—"

"He had some work to do, I think—or he might have had to meet an author who lives nearby. The point is, James, he was going to phone me at nine o'clock in the evening, but he didn't. Anyone who knows him will tell you how strange that is. If Oswald says he'll do something, that's it: it's done. I wish to God I'd gone down there last night."

"You couldn't phone him yourself?" Dougal said.

Victoria Yarpole looked surprised, as if the sofa she was sitting on had made a contribution to the conversation. "How could I?" she demanded. "The cottage isn't on the phone."

"So you drove down this morning," Hanbury went on, "as arranged. Mr. Finwood's car was in the garage, and his luggage was in the house. He had made up a bed but there was no sign that he'd slept there. Have I got the details right?"

"You can imagine how I felt." Victoria Yarpole put down her empty glass and picked up a small jade cat that was sitting on the same table. "I did what anyone would do—I went straight to the police. The nearest town is Kington—I went there. And, do you know, they practically told me I was wasting their time. They kept wanting to know what my *status* was."

She put the head of the cat in her mouth and sucked it as though it were a lollipop, a consolation prize for the vicissitudes of life. Dougal watched, fascinated.

"Something like sixty thousand people go missing every year," Hanbury explained. "The police can't follow up every case. They just haven't the manpower, I'm afraid."

Victoria Yarpole snatched the cat away from her mouth. "Well, they should have. As far as I could see, the main reason for their lack of cooperation was the fact that Oswald and I aren't married. How puritanical can you get?"

"It is a difficulty—technically I mean: it's much easier to get answers if you're representing a spouse in these cases."

"The spouse in this case is loathsome Lesley. That's what Oswald calls her, you know. Not that she'll be a spouse much longer."

The venom was unmistakable. Dougal glanced at their hostess, who was fondling the little jade cat. Naked malice is relatively uncommon; usually it is decently clothed in hypocrisy.

Hanbury said gently: "Does Mr. Finwood ever see—ah—his ex-wife?"

"He wouldn't if you paid him. She's a little bitch by all accounts. The only way he communicates with her is through their lawyers."

Dougal cleared his throat. "This cottage—how did you get in? Was it locked?"

"Yes, but I had a key. Oswald gave it to me before he left."

"So it was he who rented it?"

"He didn't rent it—it belongs to a friend."

"Do you know who?"

She shook her head. "What does it matter? Oswald's vanished: he's probably in danger: *that's* what matters."

"In danger? Do you know of any reason why he might be in danger?"

Victoria Yarpole shrugged. "Plenty of people are envious of his success, professionally, I mean. I told you that."

Dougal knew that modern publishing was a cutthroat business but kidnapping seemed an unusually extreme expression of professional rivalry.

"It would be useful to have a photograph of him."

"I don't have any—not yet." She must have realized that this sounded strange in view of the closeness of their relationship. "I've got three rolls of film waiting to be developed. One hundred and eight shots of Oswald. I just haven't had time to develop them."

"That's a pity," Dougal said.

She stared at him for a second. Then: "For God's sake, let's have another drink."

"Would you get them, William?" Hanbury said.

They waited in silence while Dougal collected the glasses. The drinks table was just behind the sofa. He was out of sight, out of mind.

"If my father hears about this, he'll be furious," Victoria Yarpole said.

"My dear, you mustn't worry about that."

"But I do. If he knew that Oswald and I intended to spend a week together, he'd—"

"There's no reason why he should. And I'm sure we'll find there's some perfectly straightforward explanation." Hanbury leant forward and patted her hand. "You can rely on me. You know that."

"Find him for me, James. Please find him."

"I don't like it," Dougal said, half an hour later. "Why don't *you* do it?"

"You know the geography. You know the personalities. It's quite safe. I've already talked to the man on duty."

Hanbury put the Jaguar into drive and nosed down the street to the junction with Bayswater Road. He turned left, towards Marble Arch. Darkness had fallen while they were at the flat.

"Finwood can't be poor, you know," he said. "He gave her that jade cat. Must have cost a bob or two. I thought publishers worked for love, not money."

Dougal ignored this. "Why me?"

"You're not a retired flatty, like most of the others. They'd handle it wrongly. Anyway, I can trust you."

"It's not that you want a scapegoat if something goes wrong—if Yarpole finds out?"

"Don't be silly, William. If you're involved, then I am too. Everyone knows I appointed you. And listen, all we have to do is go through the motions. It's nothing to worry about."

"I need to phone Celia. She's expecting me for supper."

"Be my guest," said James Hanbury.

The phone rang as Celia was on the stairs.

She wanted to go in both directions simultaneously, up and down. Upstairs, Eleanor was crying her heart out, which made Celia think uncomfortable thoughts about cot death, choking on your own vomit and the terrible desolation that solitude must be to a nine-months-old baby. On the other hand, the health visitor had made a point of saying that the only way to get Eleanor to go to sleep at a reasonable hour was to leave her crying in her cot. "By all means check her every ten minutes," the woman had said with the unassailable confidence of a mother whose children had reached their teens. "She'll survive."

Meanwhile something downstairs was burning. It was probably the spinach lasagne. The strength of the smell suggested that Celia had seriously miscalculated when she set the timer on the new oven.

And now the phone. Celia jumped down the rest of the stairs, skidded on the rug in the hall and burst into the kitchen. Visibility was poor. She switched off the oven with one hand and seized the handset of the phone with the other. Then she retreated coughing into the hall, closing the door behind her.

"Celia—it's me. Are you okay?"

The answer to that was no. "Just a few domestic crises," she said. "Nothing to worry about."

"I don't think I'm going to make this evening. I'm sorry. But—"

A burst of crackling drowned what William was saying. A carphone, Celia thought, which probably meant that he was still in the Jaguar, which in turn meant that Hanbury might be eavesdropping.

". . . and I don't know how long it will take. Could I come round on Tuesday evening instead?"

"I'll be in Birmingham," Celia said. "A trade fair."

"Who'll look after Eleanor?"

"The nanny, of course. Anyway, that's my affair."

There was a silence on the other end of the line or maybe it was a quieter form of interference. Upstairs, Eleanor's sobbing was increasing in volume. Why did no one ever mention that having children made you feel almost permanently tired, guilty and inadequate? Celia wanted to shout at someone, preferably William. But she knew she had been unjust, that Eleanor was his affair as well as hers. For Eleanor's sake she tried to make amends.

"William?"

"What?"

"Could you manage tomorrow instead?"

"I don't know. I'll try."

"All right. About six? You can bath Eleanor."

His reply was drowned by a roar of static or whatever they had on carphones. Celia put down the phone and went upstairs to Eleanor.

"I shouldn't be doing this," Mr. Fisher said as he led the way up the stairs. "Has Mr. Hanbury cleared it with Mr. Yarpole? I mean, company security, that's Mr. Yarpole, isn't it? You can't deny that."

Fisher looked like an old soldier, Dougal thought—probably a retired NCO like most of the older employees of the Company Security Division. At a guess he wanted something more than the thirty pounds that Hanbury had slipped into his hand. Dougal proceeded to give it to him.

"Routine inspection is covered in Article Five of the contract—

Sub-section D(iii) to be precise. D(iv) allocates responsibility for it to Mr. Hanbury's division."

"I've never come across a routine inspection before. Not in this job."

"Well, you wouldn't have done necessarily," Dougal said. "That point is dealt with in Article Eight and in the Addendum. The inspections are routine spot-checks, not routine practice for every firm. I mean they're routine insofar as they're part of *our* routine as opposed to your routine or the company's routine." He added, a little desperately: "And with routines like that, of course, the whole point is the absence of routine. Otherwise it'd be pointless."

Fisher stopped and looked down at Dougal. His face was flushed above the dark blue Custodemus uniform.

"Has someone been complaining? Is that it? Why don't you just come out and say so?"

Dougal marvelled, once again, at the tendency of people to listen to their own emotions, rather than to what was actually said to them; it was true, however, that Fisher had some excuse because even Dougal hadn't understood what he'd said.

"Not at all," he replied. "The routine is designed to safeguard *us,* you see. Our insurers insist on it. You wouldn't believe how devious some companies can be. Head Office needs to make sure that we're protecting what we've been hired to protect. If there's a sackful of bullion up there, they want to know. In effect, we're checking on the company's honesty, not yours. It's not just that, of course. I also advise on the O and M angle."

Fisher snorted and, unenlightened but partly appeased, carried on up the stairs. Gasset and Lode occupied the top two floors of a plain, eighteenth-century house in one of the smaller streets that run parallel to Piccadilly and east of Old Bond Street. The inside had been renovated so often that there was little to show it wasn't a modern building. Gasset and Lode was a division of Humphrey Phelps and Sons, and another division of the same company occupied the first three floors of the house. Phelps, of course, was a wholly-owned subsidiary of a large American publishing house, which was itself a relatively unimportant part of a multinational media corporation. The corporation itself was controlled by an Armenian who had been born in Sofia, educated in Vienna and had served without distinction in the French Army; he was, for the time being, a Canadian citizen.

"Well, here we are," Fisher said. "Gasset and Lode. I'll have to stay, you know. Just to keep an eye."

The centre of this floor was given over to an open-plan office where the secretaries, a copywriter and a desk-editor worked. There were four other offices, two at either end.

"I was wondering if we could have a cup of tea," Dougal said. "No point in being uncomfortable, is there?"

Fisher nodded. He went into the tiny kitchen by the lift. Dougal pulled out a notebook and walked quickly into the largest of the individual offices, the one that belonged to the publishing director; it had a cast-iron Victorian fireplace whose sole function was to demonstrate its owner's importance.

The room was full of books—typescripts, proofs and finished copies. They had long since overwhelmed the steel shelving that lined two of the walls. Piles of them had marched across the carpet and taken possession of the desk. Another column had encircled and covered the coffee table.

Even the walls had succumbed to the onslaught of literature: they were papered almost entirely with cover proofs and posters. One poster was draped over the electronic typewriter on the desk. It showed an American eagle with a scantily-clad woman suspended decoratively between its claws. Below this arresting image was a pleasantly unsubtle caption: *EMPIRE OF FLESH AND BLOOD. CAN YOU AFFORD TO MISS IT?*

Dougal went through the drawers of the desk, none of which were locked. Their contents offered an unexpected contrast to the rest of the office. Everything was in its place and everything was tidy. One drawer for stationery, another for expenses; a third for sales figures and a fourth for the agendas of editorial meetings. One drawer contained nothing but an empty can of Diet Coke and a few crumbs.

The desk diary was in the shallow central drawer. Dougal turned to last Friday. Finwood had had an editorial meeting in the morning, followed by lunch with an agent and a meeting with Graham Grimes, the chief executive of Phelps, in the afternoon. The handwriting sloped slightly to the left; the ascenders and descenders were long and ragged, like the branches of a fruit tree in need of pruning; but the centres of the letters looked as if the writer were trying to compress them. The effect was contradictory and unsettling.

Yesterday, Saturday, had a number of entries too. "Ed—keys" might refer to the keys of Sheba's Tump. Another, in red Biro, said "McQ??!." A third, barely legible, was potentially the most interesting: it looked like "Lesley 12:30," and it was followed by a phone number; Dougal didn't recognize the STD code, but it was certainly outside London.

He skimmed through the pages into the future. In the following fortnight, each day was marked "Holiday" in a way that reminded Dougal of a child's diary. On Monday week, during his holiday, Finwood had an appointment with someone called Ralphson at 10:15. The following Monday Finwood would be back at work: during that week he faced a launch party, a sales conference, two business lunches and an evening of unspecified jollity at the Groucho Club.

Dougal made a note of the appointments for yesterday and Monday week. A thought struck him, and he went into the open-plan part of the office. The nearest desk belonged to Finwood's secretary. The in-tray was empty apart from several typed sheets held together by a paperclip. "Sharon," Finwood had written on top in red Biro, "Do this soonest. Those marked with asterisk first. Yours, Oz."

Finwood's parting instructions ranged from "Get Valentine to send current rights breakdown for EFB to G.G." to "Reject following titles, return mss. and file A.T.'s reports. Standard letter." There was also a handwritten memo to be typed up and given to Josephine Jones, Finwood's deputy, who occupied the office immediately opposite his.

A. J. McQuarm

*G.G. agrees with me that the agent is likely to want at least £175,000
for sequel to EMPIRE OF FLESH AND BLOOD, subject to a suitable
outline. Vital to avoid auction situation. G.G. believes that (1) we
should hold out for world volume rights and (2) argue author's
reclusiveness could be turned into promotional asset. Could you find out
from Rights how much they think they'll get for U.S., translation and
paperback rights, and let me know how many copies we'd need to sell in
hardback at £13.95, paying our standard royalties, in order to match
this advance. Agent is unhappy with proposed jacket for EFB mass-
market edition—please get on to the paperback people. I hope to discuss
new book with both author and agent while I'm away. Will report back.
Cheers!! Oz.*

"Oy!"

Dougal jumped. He swung round, the memo still in his hand.
Fisher was standing in the doorway that led to the corridor where
the kitchen was. His eyes were bright with malice.

"This tea," Fisher said. "I made some. But the milk smells something terrible. Do you still want it?"

Several lighted windows relieved the monotonous facade of Custodemus House. As its promotional literature was wont to point
out, the company never slept. "Twenty-four hours a day, 7 days a
week, 365 days a year. Permanent peace of mind."

It was nearly midnight when Hanbury and Dougal arrived. Head
Office occupied a concrete box in Sussex Court, one of those little
alleys south of the Strand and north of the river. The city around it
was so drained of life that the building seemed a different place
from its daytime self: the nocturnal tranquillity of the darkened and
nearly empty streets threw the activity at Custodemus House into
unnatural and slightly sinister relief.

Hanbury took Dougal up to his office, which was on the top
floor. He had a view of the Thames and a desk that covered much
the same area as a king-sized bed. On the desk were three telephones and two VDUs. One of the night staff brought them coffee

and sandwiches. While Dougal sat smoking, Hanbury used two of the phones and one of the screens.

"That's simple enough," he said at last. "Halcombe, Gloucestershire. The address is six St. Stephen's Street. The electoral roll lists two people living there: Lesley Finwood and Louisa Kanaird."

"Is that all?" Dougal said.

"Come on," Hanbury said, offended. "It's Sunday night, remember? Give me forty-eight hours and I could probably fill you in on the Inland Revenue angle and the Social Security one too. I could check their credit status and just possibly take a look at their bank accounts. But you don't need that sort of thing. Not yet, in any case."

Dougal smiled at him. "I was only teasing." He picked a road atlas from the bookcase and looked up Halcombe. "It's more or less on the way. I could go there first. Why do you think he lied to La Yarpole about that?"

"I imagine he was being diplomatic," Hanbury said. "I don't think I'll mention that to her—not now." Suddenly he changed tack: "What about McQuarm? Did you get an address?"

"I tried, of course. No luck."

"What do you mean? They must have an address for him."

"I couldn't make a thorough search with that man Fisher breathing over me. But I checked the obvious places. Gasset and Lode have got a file for each of their authors. But they haven't got one for A. J. McQuarm."

FOUR

NOTHING, MRS. KANAIRD THOUGHT, will ever be the same again.

She plugged in the coffee machine and switched it on. Lesley and Olivia were out, and the tall, narrow house was silent. For once she failed to relish having her home to herself.

Still, when the doorbell rang she was tempted not to answer it. Mrs. Portnum, armed with a jar of her inedible marrow chutney, was almost certainly standing on the doorstep. She had threatened to call today when Mrs. Kanaird had met her in the butcher's on Friday. It is quite difficult to make marrow chutney inedible, but Marjory Portnum never failed. The chutney was intended as a bribe, in gratitude for which Mrs. Kanaird was expected to take responsibility for a stall at the next jumble sale in the parish hall. Was it in aid of the Halcombe Cub Pack or something else? Mrs. Kanaird had forgotten which deserving institution was currently in thrall to Mrs. Portnum's formidable powers of organization.

She smoothed back her hair and went to answer the door; she couldn't spend her life avoiding Marjory Portnum, much as she would have liked to. The hall was an obstacle course of toys—what could you expect with a three year old on the premises?—and she noticed again that it badly needed redecorating.

A young man was standing not on the doorstep, a practice which infuriated her, but on the pavement. St. Stephen's clock was chiming ten; it was still five minutes slow.

He said, rather nervously: "I'm looking for Mrs. Finwood. Mrs. Lesley Finwood."

"She's out, I'm afraid. Can I help? I'm her mother."

He wasn't as young as he looked at first sight: late thirties perhaps; there were bags under the eyes and a sprinkling of grey in the badly-cut hair. His trousers needed pressing and he wasn't wearing a tie; his jacket looked as if it had come from a charity shop.

"Actually, I'm looking for her husband. Mr. Oswald Finwood."

Mrs. Kanaird wanted to slam the door in his face. Instead she said: "And who are you?"

He took a card from his breast pocket and gave it to her.

CUSTODEMUS, she read. *PRIVATE INVESTIGATIONS DIVISION.* Below in smaller letters was written: *William Dougal.* Underneath that was a London address and a telephone number.

"I'm not sure I can help you," she said. "My daughter's separated from him—they're getting a divorce."

"Yes, I know. I—"

"Who hired you?"

"I understand that our client is a friend of Mr. Finwood's."

Mrs. Kanaird looked again at the card and tried a diversionary tactic, one that would take her briefly on to safer ground: *"Custodemus?* It doesn't mean anything."

"You're right."

She frowned, deciding he was probably bluffing. "It's fourth conjugation. *Custodio.* "

"Exactly," Dougal said. "Just what I thought."

"It should be *custodimus,* or possibly *custodiemus.* "

"Custodiemus? Don't you think the future tense might create the wrong impression? 'We *shall* protect'—most of our clients want it now. I suppose they could have used the present subjunctive, *custodiamus;* but that would have made the whole thing sound rather hypothetical, don't you think?"

"Do many private investigators have the advantage of a classical education?"

"Not that I know of. Nor do most of our clients. Is Mrs. Finwood likely to be back soon?"

"Fairly soon. She's shopping."

"Did *you* see Mr. Finwood on Saturday? At half-past twelve?"

"Yes," Mrs. Kanaird said. "As a matter of fact he came to lunch."

"I thought they weren't on speaking terms."

"Then you've been misinformed. He wanted to discuss the divorce, of course, and also there was the question of Olivia."

"Olivia?"

Mrs. Kanaird looked past him, to the junction of St. Stephen's Street and the Market Place.

"There's Olivia," she said. "And Lesley."

Olivia was running ahead, her red boots flashing in the sunshine. "Granny," she shouted, "I've had some chocolate."

"Mind you clean your teeth then," Mrs. Kanaird said automatically. "Or else they'll go rotten and fall out."

Lesley, who was a few paces behind her daughter, cleared her throat to express her disapproval. She and Mrs. Kanaird did not see eye to eye on many subjects, and Olivia's consumption of chocolate between meals was near the top of the list.

Olivia suddenly realized that there was a stranger in the vicinity. She hugged her grandmother's leg and looked at him with a mixture of suspicion and hope on her face. But he wasn't looking at her. He was looking at Lesley.

"This is a private investigator, darling," Mrs. Kanaird said, aware how absurd the words sounded. "He's looking for Oz. I told him he came to lunch on Saturday."

Lesley was small and dark—so dark that she had sometimes been taken for an Anglo-Indian. Today she was wearing jeans and a red and yellow jersey; she had the sort of complexion, and perhaps the personality, that could cope with bright colours. Mrs. Kanaird greatly preferred pastels.

"Well, he was here on Saturday," Lesley said. "But I don't know where he is now."

She shifted the shopping bag into her other hand. It was an old

Sainsbury's carrier and, without warning, one of the handles gave way. A half-pound bag of frozen peas, a tin of sweetcorn and a pound of mince hit the pavement. Olivia squealed with laughter.

Dougal and Lesley bent down simultaneously.

"Oh damn—"

"Let me—"

The other handle snapped. Fortunately nothing was broken. A moment later, Lesley had gathered up the shopping and piled it into Dougal's arms.

"I think we owe him a cup of coffee," Lesley said.

"Yes, of course," Mrs. Kanaird said, as if nothing could be more natural than to offer hospitality to seedy little private investigators. "Come in."

She preceded them down the hall to the kitchen.

"Let's have it outside," Lesley went on. "It's a lovely morning."

"Are you sure you want to?" Mrs. Kanaird said before she could stop herself.

"Why not?"

Dougal dumped the shopping on the kitchen table. Olivia, who had been watching him carefully, moved a little closer.

"I've got boots on," she said.

"Red boots," Dougal said. "With tigers on them."

"You haven't got boots. Have you any at home?"

"That's enough, Olivia," Lesley snapped. "Mr.—this man hasn't come to talk about Wellies."

"William Dougal," Dougal said. "And yes, I have. Got some Wellies, I mean."

"What *colour* are they?" Olivia demanded with a touch of exasperation, as if to imply that Dougal should have mentioned this at first.

"Let's go outside," Lesley said, pushing Olivia towards the hall. *"You* need to wash your hands and face after that chocolate."

"And do your teeth," Mrs. Kanaird added, a little hesitantly because Olivia wasn't her child.

"They're black," Dougal said. He turned to Mrs. Kanaird. "Can I carry something?"

"Come with me," Olivia said to Lesley. *"Please."*

Lesley shrugged, smiled—rather nicely, Mrs. Kanaird noticed—at Dougal and followed Olivia.

"With children," Mrs. Kanaird said, feeling that some sort of explanation was due, "you find yourself operating on two different levels at once. It's extraordinarily tiring."

"And with grandchildren, you operate on three, I suppose?"

Mrs. Kanaird nodded. The conversation was in danger of becoming too personal, too quickly. The man was a private investigator, not a friendly acquaintance, and he was here about Oz.

"There are chairs in the porch." She waved in the direction of the back door. "If you really want to help you could put them out. We usually sit near the plum tree."

As she put away the shopping and set the tray, she tried not to watch this potentially hostile stranger prowling round her little garden. Life has to go on, she told herself; you can't allow the past to colour the future. Nevertheless she watched him.

Carrying the chairs, he glanced at the pile of flagstones near the door, at the tiny lawn and at the high, south-facing wall where she had trained the peach tree. The wall, like the house, was built of the local oolite limestone, which varied in colour from light honey to dark honey; it retained the heat and seemed to glow even on dull days. To the right of the peach tree was a gate that gave on to the lane where they parked the car.

Dougal unfolded the chairs and arranged them round the stone slab that served as a table. He stood back, surveying the result, and then moved one of the chairs a few inches nearer the table. He cares about details, Mrs. Kanaird thought, not that it matters.

Now he was walking back to the house—sauntering and looking around as though he were an invited guest, which in a way he was. On one side was the brick-built extension to the bookshop next door, an excrescence the planners should never have allowed; at this time of year at least the bricks were partly masked by wistaria and flame-coloured Virginia creeper. Opposite was another stone wall, lower than the one at the back, but the foliage of the apple trees in next-door's garden compensated for the lack of height.

Dougal looked up at the house: at the three narrow storeys faced with dressed stone that badly needed repointing. The wall was streaked with droppings from the nests of the swallows and the housemartins. Mrs. Kanaird wished she could see the place through his eyes. Nowadays, all she saw herself was that it was not a house to grow old in: it had too many stairs and needed too much maintenance. And she couldn't even sell it because it wasn't hers to sell.

Suddenly she backed away from the window, afraid that Dougal might have seen her watching him. Was it ridiculous to feel so threatened in your own house? Many law-abiding people found the proximity of a policeman—or even a traffic warden—made them feel not exactly nervous but a little on edge, a little more self-conscious than usual; it was a well-documented phenomenon, and you would expect private investigators to have the same effect. No doubt Dougal was used to it.

He was bending down. Mrs. Kanaird spilled a few granules of the sugar she was pouring from the packet to the bowl. She raised herself on tiptoe. He was doing nothing more suspicious than stroking Heliogabalus. Hell butted Dougal's hand with his head, arched his back and waved his tail. Mrs. Kanaird disliked cats in general and Hell in particular with increasing intensity.

Dougal came into the kitchen. "It's a lovely garden," he said. "Amazingly private. You can hardly hear all that traffic in the Market Place."

Mrs. Kanaird said the first thing that came into her head: "Sometimes it gets too hot out there. Airless, in fact."

Too late, she realized what had happened. She knew that she had an irritating tendency to denigrate a possession of hers that someone else had praised. The garden was wonderful, and she loved the way it trapped the heat. The tendency puzzled her as much as it infuriated her. Why did she do it? Was it from an obscure guilt, rooted in a sense of inferiority, that she possessed something that someone else liked and might therefore desire for himself? Or perhaps it was a superstitious attempt to avert the wrath of the gods, based on the idea that perfection was a divine prerogative, and that the gods punish those presumptuous humans who attain it in a corner of their precarious lives.

"But thank heavens it's small," she said, trying to redress the balance. "I used to have a garden that was four times the size of this, and the work never really ended."

"Is that why you're paving the area near the house?" Dougal asked. "Less work?"

The smalltalk was making Mrs. Kanaird feel slightly unreal, as though she were running a temperature. "It's such a palaver," she said. "I wish we'd never started. We've put hardcore over a couple of flowerbeds and filled in the pond between them. The beds took more time than they were worth"—for an instant she saw them as they had been a few weeks ago: blazing with colour on either side of the pond with its water lilies—"and of course the pond was such a worry with Olivia. We couldn't let her play outside alone."

"Yes," Dougal said, "I see."

He carried out the tray for her. Mrs. Kanaird appreciated his good manners but found them mildly disturbing. Private investigators were meant to be brusque individuals, always in a hurry. Her hands shook as she poured the coffee. Not necessarily a sign of strain—it could well be another of those unwelcome symptoms of age. Hell, who much preferred the company of gullible strangers to that of his owners, leapt on to Dougal's lap.

Lesley and Olivia came outside—Olivia running ahead and still talking about Wellington boots; she was a persistent child. Lesley had put on a pair of sunglasses.

"When can I have some new ones?" Olivia said. "When I'm four?"

"When your feet are too big for that pair." Lesley passed her daughter a mug. "Now drink your milk."

"Will you write my name in mine, like Ross's?"

"All right."

"Will you do it now?"

"No. Later."

Olivia sat on the grass and pulled off one of the boots. "But I want you to do it *now.*"

"Olivia," Mrs. Kanaird said, knowing that this conversation, unless her granddaughter were soon diverted, would continue until lunchtime and quite possibly beyond, "Henry's still in his cot. Shouldn't you get him up and give him his breakfast?"

"Why?"

"Because he's crying. He's very hungry and his nappy needs changing."

For a few seconds it was touch and go. Dougal looked politely bewildered. Olivia scrambled up and spilled her milk on the grass. She ran into the house, shrieking, "Henry! Henry! It's all right! I'm coming!"

"Henry's her doll," Lesley said, her face expressionless behind the sunglasses. "Have you got children?"

"A daughter," Dougal said. "She's only nine months and that's bad enough. I just can't understand how people can cope with more than one—can you?"

Mrs. Kanaird sucked in her breath and then pretended to cough.

But Lesley said, quite calmly: "Opinions vary. It's either trouble doubled or trouble squared. What do you want to know about Oz?"

"I'm trying to find him. A friend was meant to be meeting him yesterday."

"The floozy?" The sweetness of Lesley's voice did nothing to rob the word of its sting.

"When did Mr. Finwood leave Halcombe?"

"I don't know exactly." Lesley appealed to Mrs. Kanaird. "About three, was it?"

Mrs. Kanaird nodded.

"Did he tell you where he was going?"

"Well, we knew that anyway, from Edgar. He was going to Sheba's Tump. But I expect you've heard about that."

Dougal sipped his coffee. "Is Edgar the friend who owns the cottage?"

"That's right," Mrs. Kanaird said. "We've known him for years. His father used to work with my late husband, in fact."

"Did you get the impression he was going straight there? Or was he going to see someone on the way?"

"If he was, he didn't mention it to me," Lesley said. "But there's no reason why he should have done. Look, what's happened? I think you should tell us what's going on."

"There's nothing much to tell," Dougal said. "Mr. Finwood's luggage is at the cottage. But he's gone. In fact there's nothing to show he was there in the first place."

"He certainly got there. He phoned us, didn't he, Mum?"

"About nine," Mrs. Kanaird said.

"I thought there wasn't a phone in the cottage."

"It sounded as if he was in a pub," Lesley said. "Probably the one in the village."

"Funny place," Mrs. Kanaird said. "The new owners have re-named it. I can never remember what it's called now."

"The something Frog?" Lesley said. "I keep wanting to call it the Incontinent Frog, but it can't be that."

"You're sure he was at the cottage?"

"Of course—that was why he rang. He couldn't find the switch for the immersion heater. He knew we'd stayed there in the spring."

"Would you mind if I asked why he came here?" Dougal leant forward in his chair, his face anxious. "I'm not trying to pry—but anything you can tell me might help. Just to give me an idea what was on Mr. Finwood's mind."

For a moment Lesley said nothing. Her mouth twitched, which surprised Mrs. Kanaird—which was itself no surprise, for she had never been able to predict what her daughter would or would not find amusing. Or indeed whom, which might be nearer the mark in this case.

"There's no secret about it," Lesley said. "Oz and I are getting divorced. It's all quite straightforward, except for Olivia. He's not very interested in her, not at present. The point is, she's exceptionally bright—we had a child psychologist do an assessment. She's already got a mental age of six. There's a lot of potential. And there's also a very real danger that a state education won't help her

make the most of herself. My mother knows the set-up round here
—she used to be a teacher. So we'd like to have Olivia educated
privately." She paused. "Which needs money."

"And what did Mr. Finwood feel about that?"

"He was surprisingly supportive. Agreed to pay fifty percent of
any school fees. He was a scholarship boy himself, and I think that
has something to do with it—he values education. On the other
hand, being Oz, he wants something in return. Specifically, he
wants a trouble-free divorce, and that's fine by me."

"So it was a perfectly friendly meeting—"

"No, I didn't say that," Lesley interrupted. "Friendly is the
wrong word: Oz and I aren't friends. It was a business meeting, and
we happened to come out of it with an agreement."

Mrs. Kanaird offered more coffee, which Dougal refused. He sat
there, stroking Heliogabalus and looking through half-closed eyes
at the peach tree.

"You've been very helpful," he said at last. "Especially as I've no
right to ask you anything. There's just a couple more things. Do
you know anything about a Gasset and Lode author called A. J.
McQuarm? For example where he lives?"

Both Lesley and Mrs. Kanaird shook their heads.

"Mr. Finwood never even mentioned him to you?"

"Why should he?" Lesley said. "Oz keeps his life in a series of
watertight compartments. Anyway he got the job at Gasset and
Lode after we separated."

"How about Ralphson? Does that ring any bells?"

"He's Oz's solicitor. He's handling his side of the divorce."

"Have you any suggestions?" Dougal said. "Anyone Mr.
Finwood might have talked to? Close friends?"

"You could try Ed Timworth," Lesley said. "He's Oz's best
friend. His only friend, come to that."

"He's the one who owns Sheba's Tump?"

"That's right. Do you want his address?"

"Please. If it's not too—"

Olivia screamed.

"Oh *God,*" Lesley said.

She ran into the house. Mrs. Kanaird and Dougal followed more slowly. Olivia was in the kitchen, stamping on the large doll whose current name was Henry. It had long, fair hair and very blue eyes, only one of which had eyelashes. The floor was covered with what looked like a small snowstorm; Mrs. Kanaird recognized the fragmented remains of a disposable nappy.

"I can't get his jersey off," Olivia snarled.

Lesley smacked her. The screams modulated from frustration to outrage.

Mrs. Kanaird winced. "I'll find the address for you. This way."

She towed Dougal away from the battlefield and into the little sitting room at the front of the house. She opened the drawer of the bureau and searched for her address book. Meanwhile, Dougal stared out of the window at the tower of St. Stephen's.

"Here it is," she said.

The screams were dying down, thank God. With a slight shock she realized that Dougal was looking not at the church but at the two photographs on the windowsill: one was of Ross and Lesley when they were children; the other was of Olivia and Nicholas.

"I'll write the address down for you," Mrs. Kanaird said loudly. He moved away from the window at last. She scribbled the address on a scrap of paper and handed it to him.

"If there's nothing else . . . ?" Mrs. Kanaird said. "I think I'd better go and give Lesley a hand."

"I must go myself." Dougal smiled at her. "Thank you for being so helpful—and for the coffee. Oh, by the way—did you notice what make of car Mr. Finwood was driving?"

"An estate, I think. Something large and grey."

"I forgot to mention—apparently it's still at Sheba's Tump."

Mrs. Kanaird frowned. "How odd." She turned abruptly away and fumbled for the door handle. "I'll say goodbye to Lesley for you, shall I?"

She ushered him into the hall and almost bundled him into the street. When she had closed the door, she leant against it for a moment to get her breath back.

Lesley came out of the kitchen. "He's gone?"

Mrs. Kanaird nodded.

"It went quite well, I thought," Lesley said. "I rather liked him."

"I wasn't expecting it to begin so soon."

"The sooner the better, maybe."

"Lesley, he said the car's still there."

Olivia burst into the hall. Her face was calm and her cheeks were dry.

"Will you write my name in my boots?" she said.

The doorbell rang. Mrs. Kanaird wanted to swear. She wanted to go to bed and hide under the quilt with a hot-water bottle. She wanted a large pink gin. She wanted to have her first cigarette in twenty-three years. She wanted Lesley and Olivia to find a home of their own.

Some of these things were impracticable; others would have gone against the grain. There was only one thing to do and she did it. She opened the door.

Mrs. Portnum was standing on the doorstep and she had a jar of marrow chutney in her hand.

FIVE

IF OZ FINWOOD had left Halcombe at three o'clock, he should have reached Sheba's Tump by five, give or take half an hour. The estimate rested on two assumptions: (a) that he hadn't gone somewhere else on the way and (b) that his navigational skills were more advanced than Dougal's.

Sheba's Tump was one of those elusive places whose locations seem wilfully designed to confuse. Dougal reached Middle Radnor before lunchtime. It took him another twenty minutes to find the cottage, which was no more than three hundred yards from the centre of the village. Victoria Yarpole had given him directions but these were less than satisfactory. He wished he had asked Lesley Finwood or Mrs. Kanaird.

At last a labourer on a passing tractor came to his rescue. The house was on a lane he had already driven along five times. It was a low building on the side of a hill; an unkempt hedge of blackberry, elder and hawthorn concealed all but the ridge of the roof from the road; and the gate, to confuse matters further, was set back from the lane and at a forty-five-degree angle to it.

The name SHEBA'S TUMP had been painted a long time before on the top bar of the gate. Half the letters were still decipherable. Behind the house the land rose, first gently then increasingly steeply, up to a ridge that was lined with trees.

Dougal backed the Ford Sierra off the road, grazing the rear bumper against the gatepost. He got out of the car and opened the gate. Two sheep were nibbling the grass by the entrance to the barn. They glanced at him and cantered round to the back of the house. On the far side of the yard was a pond, fed by a stream that flowed down from the ridge.

Sheba's Tump—the mound, or more romantically the tumulus, of the Queen of Sheba to whom Solomon gave all her desire; the Queen of Sheba would have had slanting eyes the colour of almonds, Dougal thought, and a voice like dark chocolate; and maybe she had liked bright colours too. But she wouldn't have covered her eyes with sunglasses. Damn it. He didn't want to think about Lesley. Not in that way. In any case Sheba's Tump probably derived from a phrase that meant nothing more exciting than "the hill where the sheep are."

From where he was standing he could see the whole of the frontage. The cottage, he realized, was really a "long house" where humans and animals had once lived together under the same roof. The site was on a slope. The barn where the animals had lived was at the lower end so their urine would drain away from the humans' accommodation, probably into the stream. The whole place was built of stone—even the roof, whose moss-covered tiles were graded according to size with the smallest ones at the top.

The house was difficult to date—anywhere from the sixteenth to the early nineteenth century, Dougal guessed; it was a vernacular building whose design owed nothing to architectural fashions. Timworth needed to spend some money on it: part of the barn roof had fallen in; the wall beside the front door bulged outwards; a crack zigzagged up the chimney stack; and those anachronistic metal window frames were crying out to be replaced.

A low wall with a small gate in it separated the yard where Dougal stood from the patch of cropped grass in front of the front door. He pushed open the gate and skidded on a sheep dropping. Perhaps he should have brought his Wellington boots after all. He wiped his shoe—new last week—on the grass and followed the path up to the door. He banged the knocker and waited for a long moment before trying the key.

No one came. He glanced around, first over his shoulder and then up at the blank windows. The hairs stirred on the back of his neck. He reminded himself that his business here was perfectly legitimate. The sense of being observed was almost certainly something he had induced himself. He turned the key and raised the latch.

The door opened with a creak. It gave directly on to a large, stone-flagged room that, judging by the range in the corner, had once been a kitchen. Inside, the air was much colder and the only light came from the half-open door and a small, north-facing window. Six chairs were grouped around a pine table in the centre. The carver at the head was pulled out and at an angle to the table, as if someone who had been sitting there had just stood up and left the room.

Dougal realized, irrationally and irrevocably, that he disliked this house. It was something to do with the cold and the gloom and the misplaced chair. He didn't want to open the doors that faced each other at the back of the room. But delay was foolish: the sooner he had finished here, the better chance he would have of getting back to Celia's in time to bath Eleanor.

He tried the door on the left first. Beyond it was a large, empty room with a concrete floor and tie-beams so low that he hit his head on one of them. It was a utility area without anything useful in it, with the exception of a pair of backless leather slippers that stood on a sheet of newspaper. Immediately to his left was a door that was slightly ajar. He pushed it open, revealing a narrow kitchen like a ship's galley.

This was clean, white and modern; perhaps Edgar Timworth was a man who put his stomach first. On the counter over the fridge was a cardboard box. Dougal checked the contents quickly: a bottle of The Famous Grouse, nearly full; an unopened bottle of gin and two of claret; tea bags, sugar and coffee; tins of soup; a packet of digestive biscuits; a roll of kitchen towels; and a packet of muesli.

The contents of the fridge told a similar story: Pouilly Fuissé and vintage Ayala; milk, tonic water and lemons; a box of free-range organic eggs, wedges of Camembert and Stilton and a selection of oven-ready meals from Marks & Spencer. Dougal looked at the Chicken Tikka and realized he was hungry.

Stacked on the draining board were a plate, a bowl, a knife, a spoon, a child's mug with Thomas the Tank Engine steaming round it, a small saucepan and a glass. Dougal investigated the bin under the sink and reconstructed a meal for one person, which had consisted of lobster soup, granary rolls and cheese, washed down with Famous Grouse and instant coffee. The mug was unexpected: but maybe Olivia had left it behind. The work surfaces had been wiped down, the sink was clean and the spotless washing-up bowl was standing on its side to drain.

The non-utility room had another door, which was closed but not bolted. It led into the barn, a dark place full of dust and cobwebs. Overhead was the remains of a loft. Logs and a sack of coal occupied one of the stalls; and kindling was stacked in a manger. Keeping his head down, Dougal stumbled across the sloping cobbled floor to a low archway at the end. Grey metal glinted through the gap. Finwood's car was still here, directly beneath the hole in the roof.

The Vauxhall Cavalier was three years old. It was locked, but since it was an estate the only place where anything could be concealed was the glove compartment. The bonnet was cold and a film of dust had had time to settle on the windscreen.

His stomach rumbling, Dougal retraced his steps to the dining room and opened the other door. Beyond it was a tiny hall; on the left a flight of stairs with slippery oak treads climbed upwards in a clockwise semi-circle; in front and to the right were two more doors. The one in front led to a tiny room which was almost entirely filled by a desk and a chair. The drawers were empty. A row of books, mainly nineteenth-century German fiction and popular works on the geology of the Welsh borders, filled a shelf above the desk. Dougal opened three of the books at random and found Edgar Timworth's signature on two of the flyleaves. The owner of Sheba's Tump took his recreations seriously.

The other downstairs room was furnished as a sitting room. Dougal glanced at the first pages of a typescript on the chest beside the sofa. Nothing to do with A. J. McQuarm: it looked like a DIY manual of body maintenance with a New Age gloss: muscular mysticism. The edges of the typescript were precisely aligned with those of the table.

Someone had laid a fire in the fireplace, which was set diagonally across one corner of the room. A triangle of newspaper protruded through the bars of the grate. Dislodging the pile of coal and kindling, Dougal tugged out the newspaper. It was last Saturday's *Guardian.*

The only other item that delayed him here was a large-scale map of the area, which had been framed and hung above the fireplace. Sheba's Tump was ringed in red. Of more interest to Dougal was the village of Middle Radnor, where the letters *PH* nestled beside the church, indicating, he presumed, the pub that Lesley and Mrs. Kanaird had mentioned. There was a strong argument in favour of combining business with the pleasure of an unlimited expense account.

Dougal went upstairs and checked the bathroom and three bedrooms. One bed was made up, and there were silk pyjamas under the pillow. Finwood's clothes and a pair of shoes were neatly arranged in the wardrobe and the chest of drawers beside it. The shoes had been handmade by Lobb; maybe Finwood was a footwear fetishist like his daughter. Dougal turned them over and discovered that even the insteps had been polished. He opened the other wardrobes and the cupboards and looked underneath all the beds, just in case Finwood was also the sort to play practical jokes on his girlfriend.

The immersion heater was in one of the bedroom cupboards; the switch was on the shelf above, obscured by a pile of blankets but easy enough to find if you followed the wiring. The water tank was cold.

There was no sign of Finwood, of course; but still Dougal felt that he wasn't quite alone. If he'd believed in ghosts, he would have said the house was haunted.

It was nearly two o'clock. Dougal prayed that the pub in the village served food—preferably something more substantial than a packet of peanuts. He went out on to the landing.

As his hand touched the newel post, a bang shook the house. The front door? Running footsteps pattered down the path. Dougal dived into the nearest bedroom. The mat beneath him slid on the polished boards. He skidded across the room and landed in a huddle underneath the window.

He was too late. The window overlooked the front of the house. He could see nothing moving outside except swallows wheeling in the sky and the rump of an escaping sheep. There were no cars in the lane except his own blue Sierra. The intruder could be in the lane, concealed by the hedge; or he might have run round the house into the fields at the back.

A passing thief doing a spot of speculative house-breaking? Or was someone else looking for Oz Finwood?

At two o'clock, Lesley tried again.

This time the phone rang on; either the answering machine had been disconnected or the tape had run out. While she waited, she drummed the fingers of her free hand on the top of the bureau and watched Olivia, who was doing a jigsaw on the table.

The jigsaw had forty-eight pieces and, if she concentrated, Olivia could cope with it. The picture showed a circus ring. Olivia was trying to insert part of the ringmaster's trousers. The piece was reluctant to go in so she hammered it with her hand.

"The Timworth Literary Agency," said a high-pitched voice in her ear. "Can I help you?"

"Stop pretending to be a secretary," Lesley said. "It doesn't suit you."

"Lesley! How lovely to hear from you."

As she'd known he would, Timworth sounded both surprised and pleased. It struck her, not for the first time, that it was nice to be wanted. There were worse fates than Edgar Timworth.

"I've been trying to get you for hours," she said. "Don't you ever play back your answering machine?"

"I'm sorry—I've only just got in."

She wished he wouldn't always apologize. "Have you seen Oz?"

"No, of course not. He's at Sheba's Tump."

"That's what I thought," Lesley said, watching Olivia sweep the puzzle on to the floor. "But apparently he's not. And the Yarpole woman's hired a private investigator to find him."

Timworth squawked with astonishment. Then: "How do you know?"

"He came here this morning—the investigator, I mean. I rather liked him—he wasn't at all what you'd expect. He was asking about Oz's friends, and my mother gave him your address. I thought I'd better let you know."

"It's awfully kind of you to bother." Timworth had the irritating habit of finding kindnesses in other people's most selfish actions, and of being effusively grateful for them. "But I don't understand —Oz phoned me from the cottage on Saturday night. I was out so Rachel took the call."

Rachel was Timworth's lodger, a second cousin once-removed who worked in some ill-defined capacity for the Home Office.

"While *we* were out, you mean," Lesley said.

"Er—yes. But the point is, he must have got there. Lesley—"

"Do you know what he wanted?"

"Didn't leave a message. Actually, it's rather odd: I told him I was going out on Saturday, though not with you—he must have known I wouldn't be there. What do you think he's up to?"

"How should I know what he's up to?" Lesley said. She pretended not to notice that Olivia was kicking the jigsaw pieces under the sofa. "I've got to go."

"Can I ring you this evening?"

"Okay." Aware that this sounded lukewarm, she added: "I'd like that. And remember about Saturday, won't you."

"You can trust me," Timworth said. "You know that."

"I know," Lesley said gently. "Thank you." She put the phone down and sighed. "Olivia? Unless you've cleared that up by the time I've counted to ten, you won't be watching any television today."

• • • •

When the young man arrived at the Intemperate Frog, Mrs. Angram was polishing glasses behind the bar.

The only other customer was the retired dustman from the cottage next door; half-blind and wholly deaf, he habitually sat in front of a half-pint of bitter for two hours at lunchtime; he spoke to no one.

The young man wiped his feet carefully and walked over to her. "Hullo. Am I too late for lunch?" he said.

Mrs. Angram beamed at him. She gave him both the bar and the restaurant menus, explaining that, though the restaurant was closed, many of its dishes were available. The man bought a Perrier water and then proceeded to order the roast venison in cranberry sauce followed by chocolate mousse; he also asked if they did half bottles of champagne. When Mrs. Angram confessed that they didn't, he told her not to worry and ordered a whole bottle of Moët et Chandon instead.

She rushed the order to her husband, who was sitting at the kitchen table, trying to put new batteries in his pocket calculator. Except at weekends, when a girl from the village came in to help, Jack did most of the cooking. This was not a demanding activity, partly because there was little call for his services and partly because the cooking largely consisted of boiling frozen foods in bags and knowing how to operate the microwave oven.

When she came back the man was sitting on one of the bar stools and smoking a cigarette.

"I've got an ulterior motive," he said, laying a card on the bar. "May I buy you a drink?"

"You're a private investigator?" Mrs. Angram touched her throat with her hand. Her first thought was to wonder what mess Jack had landed them in now. "I don't know, Mr. Dougal, I really don't—I mean, I'm not sure—"

"Now please don't worry," Dougal said. "My client's hired me to trace a man who may have come in here on Saturday night. I just wondered if you remembered anything about him. I imagine you were crowded, so perhaps you don't. Anyway, how about a drink?"

Mrs. Angram rarely drank alcohol on the principle that Jack

drank enough for two or even three. Today relief made her break the rule, and she accepted a glass of dry white wine.

"What's it all in aid of?" she said. "Divorce?"

"That may come into it." Dougal shrugged. "Actually, your guess is as good as mine. The client just wants me to report back on the subject's movements. He's aged about forty, he's about six feet tall and he wears glasses. Ring any bells?"

"Whisky drinker, is he?"

Dougal nodded.

"There was a man came in about eight-thirty and asked for Famous Grouse, which we don't stock. So he had Bell's instead—three doubles in about half an hour."

"That sounds like him. What was he wearing?"

Mrs. Angram described the yellow quilted jacket and the cloth cap. Dougal congratulated her on her powers of observation.

"Did he talk to anyone?" he asked.

"No, but he made a couple of phone calls. Well, at least two. I heard him say his name, come to think of it. Fisher, or something like that."

"Finwood?"

"That's it. He didn't sound local. I put him down as a tourist."

"He was staying at Sheba's Tump," Dougal said. "Do you know it?"

"The place down the hill at the back. That explains it."

"Explains what?"

"The mud he brought into the bar. His boots were caked in it. And not just mud, either. That's why I noticed him. You'd think that people would wipe their feet, wouldn't you? You wonder if they bother in their own houses."

Jack Angram came out with the champagne in an ice bucket. He was disposed to linger and chat with this unusual customer, but Mrs. Angram shooed him back to the kitchen.

"You'll join me, won't you?" Dougal said, lifting the bottle. "I'll never finish this on my own."

She nodded, feeling that the day had slid out of her control and that she rather liked it. The old man in the corner was peering at them and looking thoroughly disgusted at such profligate behaviour.

"Cheers," Dougal said. "You were telling me why Sheba's Tump explained the mud."

"Oh that—well, I suppose he walked across the fields. People who stay there often do. It's a lot quicker than by road, and the fields belong to the cottage. Also you don't have to bother about drinking and driving."

"Yes," Dougal said, "that would explain it."

Dougal left the Sierra in the otherwise empty car park in front of the pub and walked back to Sheba's Tump.

There was a professional reason for doing so but, quite apart from that, he wanted some fresh air. Three glasses of champagne had been unwise, especially in the middle of the day. And the food he had eaten churned in his stomach: the cranberry sauce that tasted like the boiled sweets he used to buy as a child blended unhappily with the stringy venison, the oven chips, the synthetic mousse, the frozen peas and of course the monosodium glutamate and a horde of sinister E numbers.

The gate to the fields was just beyond the Intemperate Frog. Dougal walked slowly downhill, following a winding path that marked the inability of sheep to travel in a straight line. On his right was the ridge behind the cottage. Underfoot the ground was soggy and speckled with the droppings of sheep and rabbits. Today, Mrs. Angram had told him, was the first time it had stopped raining for nearly a week. If Finwood had left tracks, the sheep and the rain had obliterated them. The terrain was uneven: the fields were scattered with hummocks and dips that, despite their irregularity, had a man-made air about them. The sheep kept the grass down but they did nothing to restrict the nettles and thistles.

After fifty yards Dougal's shoes had picked up so much mud that they appeared to have doubled in weight. He was tempted to turn back before they were completely ruined. But he had been hired to trace Finwood's movements, and among them was the walk between the pub and Sheba's Tump. And something wasn't quite right—he could put it no more clearly than that. It was as if the queasiness of his stomach were paralleled by a sort of intellectual queasiness in his mind.

No doubt there was a mundane and logical reason for Finwood's disappearance, and for all of his actions on Saturday. He had an obvious motive not to mention his trip to Halcombe to Victoria Yarpole. But why settle into Sheba's Tump unless he intended to stay there? And why hadn't he phoned Victoria Yarpole from the Intemperate Frog?

According to Mrs. Angram, Finwood had made at least two phone calls. One must have been to Lesley, to ask about the immersion heater. Maybe the second phone call was the reason for his vanishing. He could have phoned McQuarm, for instance, and the author might have met him at the pub and whisked him off somewhere. It was possible; but in that case, why hadn't Finwood phoned Victoria Yarpole while he was waiting? Unless, of course, she was lying, and Finwood *had* phoned her—which of course would make nonsense of her impassioned call for help to James Hanbury. Dougal tried again: perhaps Victoria had simply misunderstood Finwood, and he had never intended to phone her in the first place.

But what about the mysterious intruder whom Dougal had disturbed at Sheba's Tump? It could have been Finwood himself, sneaking back to collect his handmade shoes. Presumably he had been hiding somewhere, perhaps in the derelict loft of the barn, and waiting for a chance to escape while Dougal was searching downstairs; it was not a pleasant thought. Maybe the intruder had nothing to do with Finwood's disappearance. But there had been no sign of forced entry, and no sign that anything had been taken.

The roof of Sheba's Tump came into view. From the back the house seemed to grow out of the hillside. Immediately behind it, at the barn end of the building, rose the largest of all the hummocks; it was higher than the house itself and criss-crossed with sheep tracks. As he drew nearer, Dougal saw that the narrow gap between the barn and the tump was filled with the tallest nettles he had ever seen.

He also realized that to reach the house he would have to climb the mound. Skirting it was next to impossible: on one side was the nettle plantation; on the other the stream that ran down from the ridge. The stream was too wide to jump.

The view from the top of the mound was superb. On a clear day like this, you could see for miles—north and west to the dark smudge of Radnor Forest on the horizon. It was a good place to smoke a cigarette. Dougal opened his tobacco tin and, his eyes still on the horizon, took out the packet of papers. The packet slipped out of his hand.

He swore. The tiny orange rectangle fluttered down between the house and the mound towards the tips of the nettles. It snagged on a fallen twig, six feet below where he was standing.

For the first time he noticed how precipitous was the drop on this side of the mound. The gap between it and the barn was like a ravine. The tops of the nettles were a good fifteen feet below him. Perhaps a previous owner had scooped out the earth to prevent the damp seeping into the walls or the mound from overwhelming the barn.

Then he saw the boot.

A glossy, green Wellington boot lay with its cream sole upwards against the side of the mound. The nettles shrouded the top of the boot.

Dougal ran back the way he had come and found a stick. He slashed at the forest of nettles. Slowly they gave way before him, though the leaves pricked and stung him—on his face, his hands and even through his trousers. As he struggled deeper into the dim and evil-smelling crack between the barn and the mound, the sour taste of nausea burned the back of his throat.

At the bottom, the ravine was only four or five feet wide. Dougal stumbled into a huge white fungus that powdered into dust. On the ground, among the yellow nettle roots, were empty tins and dead leaves, the debris of man and nature. In his haste, he gashed his hand on a rusting section of cast-iron railings; several similar sections, stacked vertically like a row of spears, lay further in.

The body was there too, as he had feared. Impaled on the railings, it looked inhuman and also unreal: a freak of nature like the fungus. The head hung upside down, nearly touching the ground; the skin of the face was discoloured by the reddish-purple stain of post-mortem hypostasis. The yellow jacket and the green corduroy trousers were sodden with rain. Mercifully, the rain had also washed away much of the blood. The eyes, bulging in their sockets, were open; the glasses, against all the odds, were not only unbroken but still in place. The mouth gaped, revealing irregular teeth the colour of parchment.

Dougal retched. He turned away and vomited against the wall of the barn.

Oz Finwood was still at Sheba's Tump.

SIX

BRASSARD-PRENTISSE COMMUNICATIONS leased two storeys of an office block in Turnham Green. Their neighbours above and below included a firm of solicitors and a firm of accountants. They employed twenty-seven people, and this year's turnover would probably pass the £2 million mark. As Hugo Brassard, Celia's partner, was wont to say with pardonable frequency, he and Celia had come a long way in the last eighteen months.

Usually Celia agreed with him. Today, however, as she edged the Volvo into the office car park, she felt that she had come a long way in the wrong direction. Behind her, at home in Kew, was Eleanor. When Celia left, her daughter had been crying.

"Don't worry, Ms. Prentisse," said Valerie Blackstick, who was tall and dark and reminded Celia of the housekeeper Mrs. Danvers in *Rebecca*. "Just leave it to me."

Celia had wanted to say that Eleanor was a she, not an it.

"A clean break is always best." Valerie Blackstick seemed to swell in the doorway, inflating herself as though to prevent Celia from rushing back into the room and picking up Eleanor. "The sooner we start the better. Believe me, I know."

Celia had lacked the confidence to break through this awesome barrier of professional competence. Valerie Blackstick's authority was backed by the highest recommendations from the agency and by wonderful qualifications; and it was somehow—powerfully if illogically—underwritten by the fact that Valerie Blackstick had demanded, and got, a salary that was a good 20 percent above the going rate.

Besides, the woman was only doing her job, and Celia had a five o'clock meeting she couldn't afford to miss. The appointment had been scheduled for weeks: Hugo was going to introduce her to a new client, whom she was meant to impress with a range of brilliant new ideas for raising his public profile. Failing to turn up might not lose them the account but it certainly wouldn't impress the client. Keeping the client happy was not only the first rule in the public relations industry but also the only rule of any importance. She was already five minutes late.

Her secretary flagged her down as she came into the office.

"Can't stop," Celia said. "Are they in the conference room?"

"No, in Hugo's office. Calm down." Judy, though ten years younger than her employer, tended to mother her. "Their MD's late, so there's no rush. But Miss Blackstick rang a few minutes ago: she can't find the clean nappies."

Celia went into her own office and collected a file from the desk. "Ring her back and tell her to look beside the chest of drawers in Eleanor's room. And remind her to use disposables."

She was sure she'd pointed out the nappies. In any case, had the bloody Blackstick no initiative?

"And William Dougal phoned."

Celia checked her face in the mirror. "What did he have to say?"

"Well, he was in a hurry. I thought he sounded under the weather." It was well known that Judy had a soft spot for William; she had been heard to remark that what he really needed was a bit of fattening up.

A man in an ultra-conservative pinstripe suit had just come into reception. Ten to one it was the missing MD.

"Yes, but what did William say?"

"Well, he was awfully sorry but he couldn't come round this evening." Judy giggled. "He said something about having to help the police with their enquiries."

"Don't be absurd," Celia snapped. Judy's mouth dropped open, and Celia said quickly: "I'm sorry."

She switched on a smile and sailed into reception, her right hand ready for action. The man was about fifty; he carried a black-leather briefcase and exuded the aura of imperial hauteur that so often distinguishes the managing directors of medium-sized companies.

"Mr. Venn?" she said, intensifying the smile. "I'm Celia Prentisse. How do you do?"

Behind the smile she wondered miserably if William was really in jail or had just been trying to brighten up Judy's day.

Two of them were standing on the pavement, a man and a woman. Neither of them was in uniform but Lesley guessed who they were and why they'd come, and her heart lurched.

The man was in his fifties, with bushy grey hair above a broad, weathered face; you could imagine him with a pipe in his mouth and a grandson on his knee. The woman, who was younger than Lesley, wore a tan raincoat and a dark brown beret that should have made her look silly but didn't.

"Mrs. Lesley Finwood?" the man said.

She nodded.

"I'm Detective Sergeant Fields." He showed her a warrant card, taking his time about it. "And this is Detective Constable Vince. May we come in?"

She took them into the sitting room. Too late she realized that Olivia had overturned her tractor and trailer on the hearthrug, with the result that the cargo of wooden bricks had transferred itself to the floor. She had also managed to decant several dozen books from the bookcase.

"I'm afraid we've got some bad news for you," Fields murmured. He sounded like a local man, something of a rarity in Halcombe, which was rapidly turning into a dormitory suburb for the provincial cities around it.

"Who is it?" her mother called from the kitchen, where she was trying to encourage Olivia to eat her yoghurt rather than make patterns with it on the table.

Lesley didn't answer. Mechanically she tried to tidy up the toys but the complexity of the job defeated her. Anyway it didn't matter.

"What is it?" she said, her head bowed.

The officers were standing just inside the door.

"Would you like to sit down?" The woman Vince had a pleasant voice, well-modulated and classless. "Shall I fetch your mother?"

"No, don't fetch her. She's looking after Olivia—my daughter."

Lesley sank into the nearest armchair because at present it was easier to follow other people's suggestions than to make her own decisions.

Fields cleared his throat. "There's no easy way to do this. We've been notified that a man has been found dead outside a cottage in Powys. You know the place, I think. It's called Sheba's Tump."

"Yes." She bit her lip. "Is it—is it Oz? My husband?"

"I'm afraid it probably is, Mrs. Finwood. We're very sorry."

What he said was trite enough but curiously he sounded as if he really were sorry—not just to be the bearer of bad news, but also that a man he had never known was lying dead sixty or seventy miles away, and that she had to suffer in consequence. You'd think, Lesley thought, that he'd have announced so many deaths to the nearest and dearest that he'd no longer care. Perhaps the police went on training courses to learn how to be sympathetic. His compassion bewildered her, and she clung to her bewilderment.

"We understand that your husband was staying there," Fields went on. "We identified his body from the documents he was carrying—driving licence and so on. The landlady of the local pub was able to confirm who he was. But of course we need to have him formally identified. I wonder if—"

The words burst out of her: "Was it some kind of accident?"

"It looks like it. We can't be absolutely sure until they've done the post-mortem examination."

"Can I get you something?" Vince said. "A glass of water?"

Lesley shook her head. "A post mortem—but how did he die? What are you trying to say? Do you mean it might not have been an accident?"

"Now you mustn't upset yourself," Fields said. "Mr. Finwood seems to have died as the result of a fall. As far as I know there's nothing particularly suspicious about the circumstances. It's just that an autopsy is standard practice in cases like this."

"Yes, of course," Lesley said.

"We've tried to get in touch with the owner of the cottage—a Mr. Timworth, I believe? Lives in London?"

"Yes—he's an old friend. Of mine as well as my husband's." That sounded awful, as if she were having an affair with Ed. "I mean we grew up together—my parents were friends of his. He's a literary agent. I can give you the address." What a stupid thing to say: they must already know where Ed lived. "He bought Sheba's Tump as a kind of holiday-cottage-cum-investment. I—"

She stopped abruptly, aware she was talking too much. Shock did the strangest things to you. She closed her eyes and saw red waves pulsing behind her eyelids. She wished that Fields and Vince would leave her alone, and that the world would stop making demands on her. All she wanted was for Olivia to be on her lap and needing, as even now she sometimes did, to be rocked to and fro like a baby.

"Would you be able to identify Mr. Finwood for us?" Fields said gently. "Do say if you'd rather not. We can find someone else to do it—Mr. Timworth, perhaps."

"No, I'll do it. Of course I will. Did you know we were separated?" Lesley opened her eyes. Her mother was standing in the doorway. "But he was still my husband, you see, when all's said and done."

When the phone rang, James Hanbury was considering his tactics for the next board meeting. His main problem was Winston Yarpole, who by now should have died or at least retired. The old man was stifling growth.

The call was on the private line.

"Mr. Hanbury? This is William Dougal." The unaccustomed formality suggested that someone was listening in. "I'm afraid there have been developments in the Finwood case. I'm ringing from the police station in Presteigne."

Hanbury listened without interruption for three minutes. Dougal had found a body in the field behind Sheba's Tump. Papers on the corpse had identified the man as Oswald Finwood. The landlady of a nearby pub had served Finwood on the Saturday night. It looked as if he had had too much to drink and, while walking back to the cottage in the dark, had fallen to his death. There would have to be an autopsy, but the police seemed not to suspect foul play. Dougal understood from them that Lesley Finwood, the estranged wife of the deceased, had agreed to make the formal identification of the body. He had explained to his hosts that Custodemus was acting on behalf of Victoria Yarpole, a friend of the deceased, who had in fact reported his disappearance to the police in Kington yesterday morning.

Well, that's all very interesting, Hanbury thought. Really rather promising, too. It could hardly be better.

Aloud he said: "This is very distressing. As you know, our policy is to help the police in any way we can. There's no time limit on this one at all. Ah—if you have the opportunity, I wonder if you could explain to them something of the delicacy of Ms. Yarpole's position; her father is not wholly rational—it may well be a case of senile dementia. I think you'll find the police may be willing to keep her name out of it. After all, she's not directly involved. Would it help if I had a word with the officer in charge of the case?"

"Yes," Dougal said, "he'd like that."

The conversation that followed was most satisfactory. Hanbury had always found the police, if handled with due care and consideration, to be eminently sensible people; and Detective Inspector Jeans was no exception. The inspector quite understood the need for discretion and assured Hanbury that, if Finwood's death was as accidental as it seemed, there was no need for Ms. Yarpole's name to be mentioned at the inquest.

After the phone call, Hanbury stared unseeingly at the Thames and thought about the next board meeting. The longterm outlook had changed, and greatly for the better. The answer lay in strategy, not tactics. He picked up the phone and dialled a number.

"Victoria? This is James. May I come round and see you? I have some news."

By the time they let him go, it was after eight o'clock.

Dougal felt as though he had been through a mangle—fed slowly through the rollers, time and time again, until all the vital juices had been squeezed out of him. He was lightheaded, and his knees trembled. He used to feel like this after a three-hour examination on an empty stomach. What did you feel like after you had been through a full-scale hostile interrogation?

The police had been the reverse of hostile. When they met him at the scene of the accident, they had enquired solicitously how he was feeling before they even looked at the body. An officer had collected the Sierra from the Intemperate Frog and driven him to the station. Here they had questioned him and then taken a statement. It had all been done in the friendliest possible way—after all, the police were dealing with an accredited representative of a reputable security company. A very young police constable had been detailed to buy Dougal some cigarette papers. Cups of sweet, milky tea appeared at the slightest provocation. While the statement was being typed up, they gave him a meal and positively encouraged him to use the phone. Later they took him back to read the statement before he signed it.

"Take your time, Mr. Dougal," Inspector Jeans had said. "We want to get this right."

There had been no conflict of interests. Indeed, Inspector Jeans had congratulated Dougal, with only the slightest hint of patronage, on the persistence that led to his discovering the body of the missing man, and on his conscientious cooperation with the police.

"It's not often we get a witness who's as helpful as you. You wouldn't believe some of the jokers we get in here—or maybe you would, being in the same line of business, as it were."

Dougal said that members of the public were a pretty mixed bunch, which seemed suitably uncontroversial.

"Some of them," the inspector said, "have the gift of the gab but they notice sod all, if you pardon my French. And others notice

things all right but they can't or won't tell you about it. Or they
don't think you'd be interested. Or they think it'll take too much
time, and there's something on the telly they want to watch. It's a
dog's life, eh? We'll be needing you at the inquest, you know.
You're not planning to go abroad or anything?''

When Dougal got outside darkness was falling from a flaming
sky. Another fine day tomorrow, it looked like, which would make
life easier for his newfound friends as they examined the ground
behind Sheba's Tump. He leant against the Ford Sierra and decided
that he couldn't face the drive back to London tonight. No doubt
the desk sergeant would find him somewhere to stay. A decent
hotel, of course: he might as well get some benefit from the bot-
tomless expense account, if only to compensate for that disastrous
lunch.

A Rover turned into the car park beside the police station. Dougal watched idly as it reversed neatly into the parking slot on the
other side of the Sierra.

Four people got out—a man and three women. Among them he
recognized Lesley Finwood and Louisa Kanaird. He had no time to
duck out of sight, even if he had wanted to.

Lesley looked at him across the roof of the Sierra. The lamps that
lit the car park bleached the colour from her face. She was wearing
dark clothes, widow's weeds for the man she had been on the verge
of divorcing. Behind her, Mrs. Kanaird gave a dry sob.

Love, Dougal thought, is the strangest thing in the world. Something in it survived the worst quarrels. There was nothing like
death for shaving away the superficial blemishes.

"I found him, you know," he said because he wanted to tell
Lesley himself, before someone else did. "I'm sorry."

"There's nothing to be sorry for," she said. "Someone had to
find him. I'm glad it happened now, not later."

The four of them marched away across the car park. Dougal
watched Lesley Finwood. To his distaste, he found himself not pity-
ing her but wondering what she thought of him.

•   •   •   •

"Celia, William's in reception. Can you spare him a moment?"

Even on the phone the concern in Judy's voice was unmistakable. It irritated Celia. There was something wistful and vulnerable about William that made certain women fall over themselves to mother him. It was beyond her why he couldn't allow one of them to marry him and sweep him away to a three-bedroomed nest in the suburbs, preferably as far as possible from Kew and Turnham Green.

"I'm busy," she said, which was true: she had to be at the Birmingham Exhibition Centre by 2:30 P.M., and she was trying to clear a backlog of paperwork before getting a taxi to Euston.

"You can spare him a couple of minutes," Judy pleaded. "He says it's urgent."

"All right," Celia said.

"Would you like me to bring in some coffee?"

"No, I wouldn't."

She stared out of the window at the rain that was thudding down on London. It was a grey Tuesday morning. The weather had shifted abruptly from summer to late autumn. Winter was coming: dark mornings and dreary evenings would make it even harder to cope with the opposing demands of work and home. She felt like an ogress for not allowing Judy to make them some coffee. Somehow she often felt like an ogress when William was around.

He was smiling when he came into the room—at her or at the memory of Judy? Judy was not only young but one of those slightly overweight and slightly underdressed blondes that men are supposed to find attractive. As his smile faded, she noticed that his eyes were bloodshot and that he hadn't shaved. His hair was dripping with rain and his new black shoes were covered with mud, some of which had already transferred itself to the carpet.

"Oh for God's sake," Celia said. She dialled reception. "Judy, we'll say yes to the coffee after all. And can you bring a towel and some paper handkerchiefs?"

"Sorry about the lack of warning," William said. "I've just driven up from Powys." He glanced down at his shoes, at the mud. "Oh Lord, can I clear that up? It was sunny in Wales. A beautiful day."

"How did it go? The case?"

"It's all over bar the shouting." He was still looking at his shoes, his forehead wrinkled in a frown. "At least I think so. I'll tell you about it later, if you want, that is. How's the nanny?"

"Is that why you've come?"

"Partly." He sat down and bent to unlace his shoes. "The other reason was to say sorry for last night."

" 'Helping the police with their enquiries'—what sort of a message was that?"

"I couldn't say much on the phone. And when I'd finished helping them, it was too late to drive back so I went to a hotel for the night."

Celia was tempted to make a sarcastic remark about the apparent scarcity of telephones in the Welsh hotels, but that would have been too revealing. Judy came in with the coffee. Dougal thanked her with a smile. Given half a chance, Celia thought, Judy would have stayed to dry his hair and clean his shoes.

When they were alone he asked about the nanny again.

"She's fine," Celia said. "A real professional."

"Does Eleanor like her?"

"It's hard to know. It's not as if she can tell me, and I haven't seen much of them together yet." Aware that she sounded defensive, she changed the subject: "But why were you helping the police?"

He shrugged. "I found a body."

"You did *what?*"

"It was the man I was looking for—the man James Hanbury wanted me to trace. He'd had an accident. Look, about what's-her-name, the nanny: I had an idea. An alternative that would be better for Eleanor and cheaper for you. Can we talk about it?"

Celia glanced at her watch. "I'm sorry—it'll have to wait." She picked up the phone again, glad to have an excuse. "Judy, is the taxi there?" It was. "I've got to go."

"Oh well." William smiled at her and before she could stop herself she was smiling back. "It'll wait till Sunday."

"I can't manage Sunday. We're going to stay with Margaret."

She stood up and gathered her belongings together. Margaret was her stepmother; she and William had never got on. "How about Monday evening? I'll try and get off work early."

"All right," he said. "Look after yourself."

And suddenly he was gone, leaving a half-drunk cup of coffee, a damp towel on the arm of his chair and a pile of muddy tissues in the waste-paper basket. Celia closed her briefcase with a snap. She had a fairly good idea what he wanted to suggest; but she didn't want to hear it now. The trouble with William was that you couldn't rely on him. He conducted his life according to some private code whose dictates were completely unpredictable. She had learned that the hard way and it wasn't the sort of lesson you forgot.

But as she left the office, smiling with guilty warmth at Judy in reception, she wondered if she were doing the right thing. Not for herself or for William, of course: for Eleanor.

SEVEN

"PASSING ON IS A BUSINESS, like any other," Athelstan Finwood croaked, spraying flakes of vol-au-vent pastry over the shiny lapels of his black suit. "Big business, too. You know what all that cost?"

Dougal said that he was afraid he had no idea. Suddenly he realized why he found Oswald Finwood's sole male relative so unsettling. Athelstan's face was thin—his cheekbones were sharp points on the verge of breaking through the dry, pale skin that covered them; but his lips were thick, red and flabby. A voluptuary's mouth in an ascetic's face.

"Well, I have," Uncle Athelstan said with a trace of asperity, as though Dougal had tried to contradict him. "I asked the undertaker. Nine hundred and forty-three pounds. And that's just the actual burial, the basic package. The coffin, the hearse, the crematorium fees and so on. It would have been more if we'd had a clergyman and all the trimmings. It's a scandal."

Dougal began to edge away. No one else had shown the slightest desire to talk to him but even self-conscious isolation was preferable to the company of this dreadful old man.

"I bet they didn't even bother with getting quotes from more than one firm." Uncle Athelstan took a step to his right, ostensibly to lay his empty plate on a table but really to cut off Dougal's retreat. "They should have buried him in Wales, if you ask me. It would have been much cheaper. Or they could have done it in Halcombe. My nephew wouldn't have minded—he'd have approved: he watched the pennies, Oswald did. He was nobody's fool. So why did they bring him all the way back to London?"

"I suppose because he lived in London," Dougal said. "And all his friends are here."

"Not many of those," Uncle Athelstan said with a certain sardonic pleasure. "Mind you, we Finwoods have always kept ourselves to ourselves. We're a dying breed. Do you know, apart from Olivia I'm the last of the family? Who'd have thought it? My father was one of thirteen. The way things are going, I'm going to outlive them all. First Nick, then Oswald. It's like there's a curse on us."

"Who was Nick?" Dougal said, a memory stirring in his mind of a photograph on a windowsill.

"You don't know?" Uncle Athelstan's face was suddenly suspicious. "I thought you were a friend of Oswald's. Who are you? Some damned reporter?"

"No, of course not. I work in publishing."

"You don't say. Well, in that case I'm the Sheikh of Araby."

Athelstan Finwood tottered away. Earlier he had confided to Dougal that he was a retired debt collector, which perhaps explained his cynical view of human nature.

Dougal glanced around the room. With an astonishing generosity that smacked of relief, Gasset and Lode had underwritten the cost of the reception after the funeral. They had hired a private room in a hotel that was conveniently near the St. Pancras and Islington Cemetery; they had provided taxis from central London and arranged the catering. The gesture would not be excessively expensive because there were few mourners.

Most of them had been colleagues first and friends second—if indeed they had been friends at all. Perhaps a dozen publishers were standing around Josephine Jones, the unofficial hostess since Gasset and Lode was footing the bill, at the end of the room near the makeshift bar. Mrs. Kanaird and Lesley Finwood were sitting in silence with a tall, thin man in his forties between them. Athelstan Finwood joined them: he jerked a thumb at Dougal and Mrs.

Kanaird shook her head. No doubt Dougal had just been exposed as a liar for telling part of the truth.

Near the door stood James Hanbury supporting Victoria Yarpole, tragic in the very simplest of black outfits. Her yellow hair was masked with a scarf. She was staring with venomous concentration in the general direction of Lesley Finwood and Mrs. Kanaird. She no longer looked like Boadicea but one of those sinister females in Greek mythology—Medea, perhaps, in one of her more malignant moods.

Hanbury was here because Victoria Yarpole was here; Dougal was here because Victoria Yarpole had insisted on it and Hanbury was paying him to come. As Dougal watched them, Hanbury murmured something in Victoria's ear: courtship disguised as consolation.

The idea disgusted him and he turned away. He found himself looking at Lesley again and wondered uneasily if his disgust at consolation-as-courtship had been directed at himself rather than Hanbury. She was wearing a navy-blue suit that discreetly advertised her figure. Dougal would have liked to have talked to her; but he didn't know what to say and in any case he lacked the courage to approach while Athelstan was standing guard over her.

To his relief Josephine Jones waved to him and he went to join her. She was a large woman, a few years older than he, who favoured loose, flowing clothes and who was never seen without a large canvas shoulder bag that had originally been designed to carry fishing tackle.

"I didn't know you knew Oz," she said.

"It's a small world," Dougal pointed out.

"Were you a *friend* of his?"

"Not exactly."

"I see. Poor old Oz. Practically everyone here has been speaking ill of the dead."

"You surprise me," Dougal said. "I don't think I've heard anyone mention him except his uncle. Everyone else seems to be treating this as a working funeral."

"Well, that's modern publishing for you. No time for sentiment or the social graces." Her broad face cracked into a smile. "No time for reading, come to that. Books—I ask you: who wants them, eh?"

"How are things going at Gasset and Lode?"

"Chaos. Absolute chaos," she said cheerfully. "Oz left a mass of loose ends and I'm going frantic trying to tie them up. Do you want some work?"

"What sort of work?" Dougal said cautiously. When publishers asked you to work for them it normally meant reading. Reading fees were derisorily small—usually a fixed amount of money that took no account of the time you had to spend reading and writing reports on books that were, nineteen times out of twenty, better left unread.

"You remember the Yorick job you did?"

Dougal nodded. Eighteen months earlier, he had earned a respectable flat-fee for tidying up the memoirs of a dead rock star. Gasset and Lode had rejected the book when the author was alive; but his spectacular suicide had made him unexpectedly commercial.

"Well, this is the same sort of thing but more so. One of Oz's little miscalculations, between you and me. It's the autobiography of a child-killer—a woman—she's just come out of jail. You'd think anyone could make the slaughter of nine little innocents tolerably interesting, wouldn't you? Especially when two of the kids were hers. But the typescript is about as thrilling as a shopping list in Esperanto. Oz paid a fortune for it so we have to do it. Interested?"

"Sounds fascinating," Dougal said.

"Can you come and see me tomorrow and talk about it?" She opened her bag and produced a diary. "The typescript was meant to go to the printers last week. Typical bloody Oz. How about lunch?"

"Fine," Dougal said. Tomorrow was Tuesday, usually a Custodemus day, but it was free because he was working today.

"Let's make it ten to one at the office. Now I suppose I'd better go and make clucking noises at poor Lesley, not that she's making an unseemly show of grief. Do you know if that's her mother with her?"

"Yes, it is. Who's the man that's with them? The younger one, not the uncle."

"Edgar Timworth." Josephine chuckled. "He used to be the poorest literary agent in London, which is almost a contradiction in terms. I want a word with Master Edgar. He owes me an outline."

She sailed off, swinging her shoulder bag like a flail. Dougal glanced from her to Lesley Finwood. This time she was looking in his direction and their eyes met. She looked away.

Hanbury beckoned him. As Dougal drew nearer he realized that Hanbury was supporting Victoria Yarpole actually as well as figuratively. She was leaning against the wall, her eyes glassy and her breath smelling strongly of peppermints.

"Give me a hand," Hanbury whispered. "Take her other arm."

"Shouldn't we say goodbye to someone?" Dougal said, not because he thought they should but because Hanbury was normally such a stickler about the formalities.

"Not on this occasion," Hanbury said. "We have no—ah—status."

They manoeuvred Victoria Yarpole through the door, along the corridor and down the stairs. She seemed capable of supporting most of her weight but incapable of directing her limbs. But in the lobby she turned her head and focused on Dougal.

"James said it was you who found him," she said with unexpected clarity. "Is that true?"

"Yes."

"Into the car," Hanbury said.

The Jaguar was on the forecourt. Panting slightly, Hanbury lowered Ms. Yarpole into the front passenger seat and strapped her in.

"I'll take her home," he said to Dougal. "Can you meet me in the office about four?"

"No," Ms. Yarpole said. "I want him to come with us."

"But Victoria—"

"I want to hear everything. Just as it happened. I want to hear about—about that woman."

"All right," Hanbury said. "Whatever you want, my dear." He

glanced at Dougal, his face hard. "Well, what are you waiting for? Get in the back."

Hanbury listened with half an ear to the conversation and tried not to let his irritation show. Victoria and Dougal were sitting on the sofa side by side, almost touching, ignoring him completely. Their coffee, which Hanbury had been despatched to make in the kitchen, was getting cold.

It should have gone very differently. He had envisaged himself driving Victoria home and staying for one of those confidential little chats she appeared to enjoy so much. Too bad she always wanted to talk about Oz Finwood: given time, that would change; it was the chats that were important, not their content.

He hadn't realized quite how drunk she was until the reception. There must have been a bottle in the handbag, and no doubt she had fortified herself beforehand for the ordeal of the funeral. It might have been quite embarrassing. Still, even that might have been turned to good account. Nothing advances a friendship so quickly as one of the potential friends being helplessly drunk.

Then she had developed this obsession with Dougal: or rather this need to hear everything he knew about Oswald Finwood and his family. Curiously enough, the more they talked, the less drunk she seemed.

"Describe the little girl to me," she said. "Why didn't Oswald mention he had a daughter?"

"I don't think they were close," Dougal said tactfully. "She's about three, I suppose. She's fascinated by Wellington boots."

Hanbury repressed a sigh and stared at the enlarged photograph of Finwood that had replaced the Second Empire mirror above the fireplace. He couldn't understand what Victoria had seen in the man. The photograph was a head-and-shoulders shot, taken outside a French cafe. Finwood stared down on them, smiling broadly, his eyes gleaming behind his glasses. He had a receding hairline, which gave his forehead a spuriously intellectual height. His smile revealed his teeth. Hanbury wondered whether he should get his own teeth capped. Would it make him look younger? Or would it merely create a mutton-dressed-as-lamb impression, like false eye-lashes on an old-age pensioner? It would certainly cost a small fortune. He thought briefly, once again, about Finwood's unexpected affluence.

"Tell me," Dougal said. "Did Mr. Finwood ever mention the name McQuarm to you? A. J. McQuarm?"

"One of his authors," Victoria said, yawning slightly. "Oswald had discovered him—he was going to be very big. Why?"

Dougal shrugged. "There's just a possibility that Mr. Finwood met McQuarm on the day he died. I wondered if you'd like us to check it out."

Victoria frowned at Hanbury. "Why didn't you mention that?"

"It was a mere detail," Hanbury said. "An irrelevancy."

"But how do you know it's irrelevant?"

"What happened is beyond doubt, my dear. The inquest established that."

An obstinate expression settled over Victoria's face. For the first time, Hanbury realized that she resembled her father. Emotionally, perhaps, as well as physically.

"They might have got it wrong," she said. "Have you thought of that?"

"We have to accept that Mr. Finwood is dead," Hanbury said. "It's tragic but—ah—there it is. The rest of us just have to—ah—go on living."

Victoria glanced at the photograph, as if seeking strength from it. "But I'm not sure that it was an accident. No one's been able to explain why Oswald didn't phone me on the Saturday night."

"That's a good point," Dougal said. "It puzzles me too."

"And now there's this McQuarm person. I'm not going to let it go at that. I want the *truth,* and I don't care what it costs." She leant back, passing a hand over her forehead. Suddenly her mood changed. "My head's splitting. I think you'd better leave me now."

"Is there anything I can do?" Hanbury said.

"No," Victoria said. "Just go, will you?"

On their way down to the street, Hanbury said nothing to Dougal. He was too angry. The abrupt dismissal was the final straw.

Victoria was being most unreasonable, and William was wilfully encouraging her. The way she had treated him was beyond belief. She was acting like the spoiled child she was, making impossible demands.

In his haste to get Victoria back to the flat, he had left the Jaguar in a slot reserved for residents' parking. DO NOT ATTEMPT TO MOVE THIS, said a notice on the windscreen. A hireling of the Metropolitan Police had attached a yellow metal clamp to the rear offside wheel.

Hanbury swore.

Dougal said quietly: "We can get a taxi on the Bayswater Road." He set off down the street.

"I've had enough of your suggestions for one day," Hanbury said.

"In a way she's right," Dougal said, "though not for the right reason. This business isn't over." He stopped and looked up at Hanbury, who suddenly felt an inexplicable twinge of fear. "If you've got designs on her, James, you really can't afford to drop the case. And there's another thing: if you're afraid of scandal, I'd keep the police out of it."

"Do you think you could possibly use plain English?"

"Okay. You saw the photograph of Oswald Finwood?"

"One could hardly miss it."

"That's not the man I found at Sheba's Tump."

EIGHT

"WHEE . . ." Holding Eleanor under the armpits, William lowered her until their eyes were level. "Bump."

She chuckled at him and opened her mouth, showing four teeth.

"Dada," she said.

"Do you think she means me?" William said.

"Perhaps." Celia was secretly annoyed that Eleanor hadn't managed to say "Mumma" yet. "On the other hand she calls most things 'Dada.'"

He passed Eleanor to Celia for the ceremony of the last feed. Eleanor had solids during the day; but at night she still insisted, to Celia's secret delight, on having her mother's milk. The three of them were in Eleanor's room, sitting on the bed that was waiting for the time when she would have outgrown the cot. Through the walls came a gentle thudding, which Celia recognized as the bass pattern of yet another twelve-bar blues.

"Muddy Waters," William said with an air of satisfaction, as if he had just found the answer to a question that had been puzzling him for some time.

"Valerie especially likes the early Rolling Stones," Celia said. "But she doesn't mind what it is as long as it's rhythm and blues."

"So you're on first-name terms now. What does Eleanor think about rhythm and blues?"

"She seems to like it too. I wish I did."

"It's a small price to pay for perfection."

She glanced sharply at him. William had been here for a quarter of an hour. Up to now, neither of them had mentioned Valerie Blackstick.

Eleanor came off the breast and grabbed her father's finger. It occurred to Celia, not for the first time, that life would be much easier for all three of them if their daughter did not so obviously like her father. William leant closer, pulled by Eleanor. His shoulder touched Celia's.

This is how it should be, Celia thought as she looked at William's dark head and Eleanor's fair one; this is how it might have been. She remembered the day when she had discovered that she was pregnant. On the same day she had been forced to accept that William, her baby's father, had his own elastic standards of right and wrong. So goodbye, happy families; hullo, single parenthood.

She and William kissed Eleanor goodnight. Celia lowered her into the cot and covered her up—an activity that Valerie Blackstick described as "putting baby down," an alarmingly sinister phrase. Eleanor kicked off her duvet, rattled the bars of her cot and screamed.

"We'll give her ten minutes," Celia said, enjoying the worried look on William's face. "Let's have a drink."

He had brought some wine, an Orvieto Classico, which was cooling in the refrigerator. There was a curious smell on the stairs and the kitchen was thick with steam. Blackstick's lentil casserole was coming along nicely, if that was the right word. Celia fetched the bottle, corkscrew and glasses and took them into the sitting room.

"You look a bit better than you did on Tuesday," she said. "What have you been doing?"

"I went to a funeral today."

Celia opened the wine, conscious that he was watching her. "Finwood's?" The inquest had rated a brief mention in the *Standard* last week.

He nodded.

"I thought that was over and done with."

"Well, it's not."

"You were going to tell me about it."

"It's not as straightforward as I thought it was," he said. Without warning he changed the subject: "You don't like her much, do you?"

"Who?" she said, knowing perfectly well. She passed him a glass of wine.

"The nanny. You—"

"Ssh."

Celia had heard the footstep outside. The door opened and Valerie came into the room. Celia felt a stab of anger. She hated having a stranger in the house—stinking out her kitchen, destroying her privacy and (for all she knew) warping the growth of her child. Valerie Blackstick looked first at William and then at the wine—disapprovingly, Celia was sure, though immediately afterwards she censured herself for being paranoid.

"You don't mind if I eat in the kitchen, do you? I can't stand food smells in a bedroom."

"Not at all," Celia lied, realizing that this had become a nightly routine, that nanny's training had already extended itself from her charge to her employer. "By the way, this is William Dougal—Eleanor's father."

"Pleased to meet you," Valerie said, backing out of the room. "Well, I'll leave you to it."

"Mrs. Danvers in her youth," William said. "Hitchcock's *Rebecca.*"

He had always had that knack of producing one of her thoughts as his own, creating the fatally alluring illusion that their minds were similar in all other respects. She wondered if he remembered their going to see *Rebecca*—years ago at the Arts Cinema in Cambridge, before everything had started to go wrong; they had held hands in the back row and Celia had wept and William had made her laugh through her tears.

"Valerie's invaluable," she said. "I can even have two free evenings a week if I want them."

"When's the next one?"

"Wednesday."

"Would you like to come to dinner at the flat?"

She agreed, hoping that he had been diverted from the subject of Valerie Blackstick.

But William said, "What we're really talking about is Eleanor. Not you and me or even Mrs. Danvers. It can't be good to leave her in the care of a stranger for most of her waking life."

"I don't have any option." Celia was suddenly furious. "I've got to earn us a living, remember? Anyway, I *like* working."

"I'm not denying that. But there is another option. No, just listen for a moment. I only have to be away from home three days a week, and I could probably juggle those days at a pinch. You wouldn't have to pay me a penny. If you'd let me, I'd sell the flat and come and live here—pay you rent."

"You?" Her surprise was so obvious that she knew it must seem cruel. "Come and live here?"

His lips tightened. A moment later he went on in the same low, reasonable voice: "Think of it: a permanent babysitter. It'd be good for Eleanor. Good for all of us."

"No. It wouldn't work."

"Why not? Isn't it worth a try?" He hesitated and said, very softly, "I'm not asking for anything else."

Both of them sat sipping their wine while the silence grew around them. *How dare you?* Celia wanted to say. The warm, familiar sitting room felt like a prison. Pans clattered in the kitchen as Valerie's preparations approached their climax. Only the crying upstairs offered a means of escape.

She got up. "I'll just check Eleanor."

On the stairs she clung to the banister for thirty seconds and told herself that she was overreacting. The immediacy of Eleanor's anguish forced her to move on. One advantage of children was that they took emotional precedence over you; you dealt with their problems before yours.

William was pouring more wine when she returned to the sitting room.

"Let's forget it," he said. "Do you want to hear about Finwood?"

The suggestion that they should forget the proposal perversely made her want to discuss it. Instead she asked why the case wasn't as straightforward as he had thought.

"Because someone's lying," William said, "or at least mistaken. Our client is a woman called Victoria Yarpole. She and Finwood were having an affair. But the man I found, and who was identified as Finwood by Finwood's wife, doesn't look the same as the man Yarpole knew. There are other things, too. I think the man I found might not have died by accident, or at the very least that someone found his body before I did."

"So one of the Finwoods was a fake?"

"That's one possibility. Just to complicate the situation, the Yarpole woman is the only child of the founder of Custodemus. James Hanbury wants outright control of the company, and the easiest way he could get it is through her. And Finwood was in his way."

Celia tried to concentrate on what he was saying; it all seemed unreal in comparison with what was happening here, between herself and William.

"You're not saying that Hanbury had a motive for killing him?"

She meant the question as a joke but to her surprise he took it perfectly seriously.

"He certainly had a motive. And I'm still on the case because Yarpole insisted—Hanbury himself wanted to draw a nice, neat line under it."

"Come off it," Celia said, thinking of the ageing charmer who had drunk China tea in the very chair she was sitting in. "I can't see someone like Hanbury *killing* someone. He's not the type."

"How do you know?" William said; and she remembered that he knew Hanbury far better than she did. "Anyway, I don't think there is a type." He shrugged and smiled at her. "But it's only an idea. After all, there's nothing to show that Finwood is actually dead."

On Tuesday morning, Dougal wanted to go directly to Halcombe, armed with one of Yarpole's photographs of the man she had known as Finwood. It was the obvious thing to do, and Hanbury wouldn't let him do it.

"Really, William," Hanbury said. "You surprise me."

The reasons he gave for refusing were at least superficially plausible. It would be difficult to get hold of a photograph without letting Victoria Yarpole know why they wanted it. Victoria, always highly strung, was at present wrought up to such a pitch that there was no knowing what she would do if they told her the truth. Hanbury rather fancied that she might nip down to Halcombe in the Ferrari with a blunt instrument in the boot. There was also an argument in favour of gathering as much evidence as they could before taking the irrevocable step of confronting Lesley Finwood and Mrs. Kanaird. Once they had talked to Lesley, anything might happen.

Dougal guessed that Hanbury had other reasons for delay. Perhaps they were relatively innocent—for example, the struggle for control of Custodemus: if the chairman's daughter were publically involved in what transpired to be a murder case, the effects at board level would be incalculable; and if Hanbury wanted to marry the chairman's daughter, he would naturally want to know as much as possible about the character of his intended wife. Another point was that direct confrontation was, as Dougal knew to his cost, foreign to Hanbury's nature. Given a choice, Hanbury preferred to make things complicated. Just as some people have a God-given talent for simplicity and clarity in thought, word and deed, Hanbury had a God-given talent for being devious.

Yet Dougal could not ignore the possibility that underlying these reasons was another, far more sinister one. Hanbury was a poacher turned gamekeeper: before he had turned to the security business, he had been a man for whom arranging a death presented few practical difficulties and fewer moral scruples. Men like Finwood had been killed for far smaller stakes than the control of a company with a turnover running into tens of millions of pounds.

On the other hand Dougal liked Hanbury and he also liked the job that Hanbury had given him. A mild and perhaps ill-founded suspicion, it seemed to him, was an inadequate reason for destroying what might almost be called a friendship and for losing your main source of income. But it did justify taking a few precautions, which was one reason why Dougal had told Celia something about the business.

"Forget about Halcombe for the moment," Hanbury said. "You can be more useful elsewhere."

And so, on the morning after Oswald Finwood's funeral, Dougal paid a visit to Oswald Finwood's best friend.

Once again it was raining.

Edgar Timworth's flat was in an Edwardian mansion block in Earl's Court. Externally the building was in a poor state of repair, and behind the windows of many of the flats were dingy curtains, occasionally relieved by large pot-plants. Perhaps the leases were running out, or the freeholder was planning to sell, or both. It was the sort of place where the childless widows of professional men lead diminishing lives on diminishing incomes.

The communal front door opened as Dougal approached it. An elderly lady backed out, leaning on a black bicycle that was approximately the same age as its owner. The door, which was on a spring, swung back and pinned both the woman and her machine against the jamb. Dougal held the door for her with one hand and helped her move out the bicycle with the other. She didn't thank him, or even look at him, but he managed to reach the door before it closed. It was a good omen, he felt: the lock was controlled by an intercom and, given the choice, Timworth might have refused to see him.

For a moment, he watched the woman, her head bowed, pushing the bicycle along the rain-soaked pavement. She looked back at him, frowning slightly as if his good nature had presented her with a small but insoluble problem. He smiled and waved.

The hallway needed sweeping and the lift wasn't working. Dougal walked up to the second floor, past peeling paint and, on one half landing, a brown smear that looked like blood. He rang the bell of Number 29. The door lacked a spyhole—another sign that Providence was on his side.

A chain rattled and the door opened a few inches. Timworth

looked down on Dougal. His face was drawn and he had cut himself shaving. His jaw literally dropped when he recognized his visitor, destroying Dougal's belief that jaw-dropping was nothing more than a figure of speech.

"Go away," he said. He shut his mouth with a snap and began to close the door.

Dougal rammed his briefcase into the gap.

"I'll call the police," Timworth said. "You've got no right to do this."

"I've come about Lesley."

"What do you mean?"

Dougal pretended to misunderstand. "Lesley Finwood. Widow of Oswald. You were talking to her at the funeral yesterday."

"Where *you* were pretending to be in publishing, I'm told."

"I do freelance work," Dougal said. "Ask Josephine Jones if you don't believe me."

"But Lesley said you're a—"

"That's true, too." Dougal took a Custodemus card from his top pocket and passed it through the gap. "All right?"

"No, it's not all right. I want you to go away."

"I'm trying to help Lesley Finwood," Dougal said, sensing that he was in danger of losing whatever initiative he had once possessed.

"I don't think she needs help from people like you. Now let me—"

"Even if her husband was murdered?"

Timworth relaxed his pressure on the door. He was frowning but he didn't go through a repeat of the jaw-dropping performance. What did that mean? That he wasn't surprised?

"You'd better explain that," Timworth said at last. "There's a law of slander in this country."

"I will explain it if you'll let me in." Dougal decided not to point out that he hadn't slandered anyone yet. "Unless you'd rather discuss it in front of the neighbours."

As if to lend weight to Dougal's threat, Providence arranged for the door of the opposite flat to open. Another old woman emerged.

She bore a strong resemblance to the lady with the bicycle, apart from the fact that she was in charge of a shopping basket on wheels.

"Good morning, Mr. Timworth," she said, looking at Dougal. "Another nasty one."

Dougal hoped she was referring to the weather.

"Awful," Timworth agreed. Then, to Dougal: "Come in."

The flat was larger than Dougal had expected. The front door led to a long, windowless hall, poorly-lit with a low-wattage bulb and decorated with a drab patterned wallpaper. At one end was a sitting room, and at the other a kitchen. Three other doors gave on to the hall, all on the same side; all of them were shut.

Timworth shut the sitting room door, as if he were afraid of what Dougal might see there, and opened the door beside it. This was a large room, which had perhaps been the master bedroom before Timworth had converted it into his office. One wall was lined with shelves on which books stood in orderly rows. The desk held nothing but a telephone and a typescript. Cover proofs had been pinned to a noticeboard; one of them showed an eagle with a woman in its claws. On another table stood a cheap computer.

"Sit down," Timworth said. "I won't offer you coffee."

He obliterated the spreadsheet with two keystrokes and sat down behind the desk. Dougal wondered whether he should modify his first impression of his host, which had been based on the jaw-dropping, his silence at the reception after the funeral and Josephine's remarks about his relative poverty.

"Who are you representing? Victoria Yarpole?"

Dougal nodded. Timworth had got the idea from Lesley, perhaps —and Finwood had probably told his best friend about Victoria.

"More money than sense," Timworth said. "What's this about murder?"

"It's a possibility, not a certainty." Dougal hesitated. He had several strong cards but he wanted to keep them to himself. It was a fair assumption that whatever he told Timworth would reach Lesley in Halcombe. "You know I found the body? The boots that Finwood was wearing weren't as muddy as they should have been."

That earned another frown.

"The landlady of the Intemperate Frog," Dougal went on, "commented on how much mud Finwood brought into the bar."

Timworth picked up a Biro and tapped it on the typescript. "Oz had been lying there for nearly forty-eight hours. Most of the time it was raining. Water washes."

"Maybe. But he was lying between the mound—the tump?—and the house. You know the geography better than I do. It's very sheltered there. One of the boots was more exposed to the weather than the other. They were both pretty clean."

"He probably cleaned them himself. With shoes and clothes generally he was—well, fastidious. The sort of man who'd change his shirt if there was the slightest mark on it."

Dougal remembered the shoes with their polished insteps at Sheba's Tump. "So what you're saying is that after going to the pub he went back to the cottage, cleaned the boots and then went out again. Why?"

"Who knows?"

"It was a filthy night. Anyway, he'd have picked up a good deal of mud just walking round the house and up the mound."

"If there is a discrepancy, it doesn't seem to have worried the police."

"That's true," Dougal said. "But maybe they didn't ask Mrs. Angram the right questions. And not just about the mud."

"Mrs. Angram?"

"The landlady." Dougal decided to give Timworth a glimpse of another card in his hand. "Did you know he made some phone calls from the pub?"

"One of them was to me. I was out. My cousin took the message. What I'd really like to know is how you think all this is going to help Mrs. Finwood. Or was that just a cheap little bluff to get inside?"

"Do you think she'd enjoy being mixed up in a murder investigation?" Dougal said. "Or Mrs. Kanaird? Or Olivia? If you cooperate and I clear this up—I mean prove the death *was* accidental—then there's no problem. But if I can't clear it up, my client's going to call in the police."

"I very much doubt they'd take her seriously. Not on the evidence you've produced so far."

"Oh, there's more. For example, Finwood had promised to phone Victoria Yarpole from the pub. But he didn't. Odd, don't you think?"

"Not necessarily. Perhaps he was having second thoughts about her. Perhaps he ran out of change. Perhaps he forgot. *I* don't know. The point is, there's nothing sinister in him not phoning her."

"He made at least two calls, possibly more. I wonder if he phoned A. J. McQuarm. What do you think?"

Suddenly the Biro skidded on the typescript, rolled across the desk and fell on the floor. Timworth looked blankly at Dougal.

"I don't know what you mean."

The man's rattled, Dougal thought, and he shouldn't be. Timworth glanced at the noticeboard. Dougal decided to increase the pressure: "I understand you're dissatisfied with the artwork for the paperback edition of *Empire of Flesh and Blood.*"

"How did you know that?" Timworth snapped.

"I told you I work for publishers sometimes. I also understand that Finwood intended to contact both you and McQuarm during his holiday. In fact he hoped to see McQuarm on the very day he died. Do you think he might have phoned him from the pub?"

Timworth stood up. His eyelids blinking furiously, he towered over Dougal. He drew back his lips, exposing long, dog-like teeth. For an instant Dougal thought he was going to come round the desk and hit him.

"That's it," Timworth said. "You've wasted enough of my time with your prying. If you ask me that client of yours is just trying to stir things up. Pure malice, and you can tell her I said that. Now get out."

Dougal got to his feet. His mind split into two. One part was on the verge of panic, as usually happened when he was faced with the threat of physical violence. The other part marvelled at the effect that McQuarm's name had had on Timworth. He allowed himself to be herded out of the office and into the murky hall.

Timworth opened the front door. "I don't want you pestering Lesley, either."

"I'd like to talk to McQuarm," Dougal said. "Think about it. I'll be in touch."

"I'm not going to give you his address, and that's flat. But I'll warn him about you, I can promise you that. And don't try to get in touch with me again."

"By the way," Dougal said as he reached the relative safety of the communal landing, "what were *you* doing on the night that Finwood died?"

NINE

"YOU CAN USE OZ'S OFFICE, if you want," Josephine Jones said. "I haven't moved in there yet. I won't be long. Just a couple of phone calls."

The Jones regime had already had its effect on Gasset and Lode. The new publishing director had left her mark on the main office, which was noticeably tidier than it had been on Dougal's last visit, the night after Finwood's death. She had also made an attack on the chaos in Finwood's room: three black plastic sacks of rubbish were standing just inside the door, the typewriter had disappeared and the population of books, proofs and typescripts had decreased dramatically.

Dougal sat down in the chair behind the desk and flicked through the typescript that Josephine had given him. The title, *Suffer the Little Children,* was thoroughly tasteless in view of the subject matter, which was perhaps a commercial point in its favour. Legibility was the first problem—the book had been printed in draft mode on a dot-matrix machine, using a worn-out ribbon. He deciphered the first paragraph:

It was a clear April day with a few, puffy, white clouds like cotton wool in the blue sky and the first signs of Spring blossoming from the trees in the park, that I was sitting knitting on a bench near the band stand where my uncle John used to play the trombone on Sundays in summer. It was a matinee coat for my sister's youngest I remember, who lived in Nottingham and was due in May. On the pond I noticed a little girl all dressed in pink feeding the ducks, on the pond. That's how it began. How could I know how it would end.

Dougal suspected that it would end as it had begun: with mangled syntax, repetition, irrelevant detail, idiosyncratic punctuation and rather less narrative drive than *Finnegans Wake*. He read on, hoping for a bit of blood or the occasional body. By the end of the third chapter he had found neither; but he now knew a great deal about the author's knitting habits and the ramifications of her extended family.

"What do you think?" Josephine said. She was standing in the doorway, armed with her shoulder bag and an umbrella. Her raincoat resembled a small brown tent.

"Looks like a complete rewrite to me," Dougal said.

"We don't have the time. Couldn't we get away with line editing?"

"You could. But you'd have to sell it on the jacket alone."

"It's been done before. Let's talk about it over lunch."

She took him to a French restaurant on Dover Street. You knew it was authentically French because the waitresses made a point of speaking broken English interspersed with *"Mais oui"* and *"Alors."* The dishes of the day were chalked illegibly on a blackboard that was invisible from most of the tables.

While they waited to be served, Josephine rummaged in her shoulder bag and produced the reader's report for *Suffer the Little Children*. The reader was even less enthusiastic about it than Dougal had been. "A natural rejection," Dougal read aloud. "File in the waste-paper basket."

"I wish we could," Josephine said. "But we're committed. Oz gave the woman an absurdly big advance, and of course the half on signature has already been paid. We'd never get the money back. It's scheduled for February, but we'll probably have to postpone publication."

They discussed the book for another twenty minutes and reached a decision that struck a fine balance between the editorial surgery needed, the time at Gasset and Lode's disposal and the amount of money Josephine was prepared to pay Dougal.

"For God's sake," she said, "let's talk about something else."

"I gather congratulations are in order."

Josephine speared a prawn on her fork. "I should have got the job last time. They ended up with a shortlist of me and Oz, and Oz sweet-talked Graham Grimes into giving it to him. Oz was quite good at that, you know. Between ourselves, Graham told me he regretted it almost at once."

"What was wrong with Oz?"

"Couldn't organize himself. Couldn't delegate. Worst of all, he had this knack of setting everyone's back up. He caused a lot of bad blood. Almost every editorial meeting turned into a slanging match. But I thought you knew him yourself."

"I only met him once," Dougal said. "And he wasn't very talkative. How come he got where he did? He must have had something going for him."

"Like I said, he was good at sweet-talking. And to do him justice, every now and then he'd come up with a real winner. If you ask me, it was more by accident than design. But he used to make out that he had this talent for spotting schlockbusters."

"Like *Empire of Flesh and Blood?*"

"Yes. No one else had the slightest enthusiasm for it. Not at first."

They ate in silence for a moment. Both of them were drinking mineral water: Dougal had ordered it, and Josephine, after a short battle with herself, had followed his lead. After his experiences at the Intemperate Frog, Dougal had decided that he could no longer cope with business and alcohol at lunchtime; it was perhaps one of the unwelcome signs of impending middle age, like the black, wiry hairs that were beginning to sprout at awkward angles from his eyebrows, and nostrils. But now he wondered if he had made a mistake to choose water. Wine and gossip go together, and he wanted Josephine to gossip.

"In point of fact," Josephine said, just as Dougal was about to risk a direct question, "I was on the verge of turning it down. Ed

Timworth sent it to me originally. He was raving about it, but he always does rave about his authors so no one takes any notice. I had one of our readers glance at it and she was the reverse of enthusiastic. But then Oz read it overnight and got quite hysterical. Memos flew in all directions. He was a great man for memos, you know, even if you were working next door."

"What's the book about?"

"Well, back in the sixties, an English hooker gets inseminated by Jack Kennedy. Then she starts up a multi-national chain of brothels. Her daughter by Kennedy has no idea what Mum does. She has a sort of jetset upbringing, quarrels with her mum about the brothels, has affairs with royalty and ends up sometime in the future as the first woman President of the United States."

Dougal blinked.

"There's more to it than that, of course," Josephine went on. "Like family feuds, the odd murder and two revolutions. But that's the gist. It's six hundred pages long so it needs a lot of plot. It was appallingly written and there were millions of factual mistakes and inconsistencies. The editing cost a small fortune. McQuarm got all the brandnames wrong and he or she obviously doesn't know the first thing about American politics."

"He or she? You don't even know—"

"Anonymity is written into the contract. McQuarm shuns publicity, apparently. As far as I know, the only people who've met him, or her, are Oz and Ed Timworth. All communications with him go through Oz or the agent. Oz rather liked it, I think—made him feel special. Actually, it's bloody inconvenient now Oz is dead. We can't even find the author file."

"Maybe Oz took it with him on holiday."

"It's possible. He was meant to be meeting McQuarm over the weekend. We're trying to get an outline for the next book. I just hope he isn't one of those one-book authors."

The anxiety in her voice made it perfectly reasonable for Dougal to ask how *Empire of Flesh and Blood* had done for Gasset and Lode.

"It's been like Christmas," Josephine said. "First the Americans took it with open arms—the Cousins." This euphemism, Dougal guessed, referred to the New York publishers who owned Phelps and hence Gasset and Lode. "The agent has sold the film rights already, to one of God's studios." Josephine's strident voice modulated into a whisper. "In fact there's a rumour that God's taking a personal interest in it."

Dougal nodded as intelligently as he could. For an instant he wondered whether this was yet another example of the publishing industry's well-known tendency to visualize itself as the nerve centre of the universe; naturally there would be theological implications. Then he realized that God was probably in-house slang for the Armenian-Canadian who controlled a substantial slice of the world's media, including Gasset and Lode.

"After that it just snowballed. Everyone wanted to get in on the act. We've scheduled it as our major autumn lead. The Japanese rights went for six figures, dollars that is, sight unseen. We've sold German and Spanish rights already. We'll probably mop up the other translation rights at Frankfurt next month. We've even had some free publicity—including the *Sunday Times,* no less."

"Nothing succeeds like success," Dougal said.

"That's what Oz used to say. He was always conceited, God knows why, but this made him insufferable. No wonder Lesley left him. The only wonder is why she married him in the first place."

"Why do you think she did?"

"Oh, in fact it's not so strange. He could be very charming if he wanted something from you, and if he thought it was worth his while. Good with women authors, as long as they were either good-looking or had good sales figures. But I imagine he was hell to live with. What really broke up him and Lesley was that business with the twins."

"Ah," Dougal said, remembering the Curse of the Finwoods and a photograph on a windowsill and deciding that it was worth a gamble. "Olivia and Nick, you mean?"

"That's it. Tragic. Oz was very cut up. He was really fond of Nick. Doted on him to the exclusion of anyone else, including Olivia." Josephine took a sip of Perrier water. When she looked up again, her face wasn't quite as good-humoured as usual. "You seem to be awfully interested in Oz Finwood."

"Oh, I am," Dougal said. "I've often wondered what makes a successful editor."

It was still raining when the taxi stopped in Burlington Gardens.

Hanbury, who had left his umbrella in the office, paid the driver and sprinted from the taxi to the northern entrance of the Burlington Arcade. The distance was only a few yards but the exertion made him pant. Perhaps he should have another check-up.

He stood at the top of the Arcade, brushing the rain from his shoulders and staring down the long cathedral of commerce to Piccadilly at the far end. As usual the tourists were everywhere, blocking the view and getting in the way of Londoners who used the place mainly as a shortcut and especially when it was raining. A beadle in grey top hat and frockcoat was posing for his photograph with a Japanese on either side of him.

"Hullo, James. You're late."

With a start Hanbury realized that Dougal was standing just beside him in the doorway of the tobacconist's.

"The traffic held me up. And something came in about Ross Kanaird just as I was leaving."

"And who's he?"

"Lesley's brother." Hanbury smiled. His heart had stopped thudding and he felt normal again. The check-up could be delayed. "Kanaird isn't a common name. I thought it might be worth our while to get the boys downstairs to run a check on it. It's amazing what finds its way on to a data base, eh?"

"Yes," Dougal said, "but is any of it useful?"

"Well, Ross isn't quite what you'd expect. He lives in Turkey but not out of choice. He'd probably be arrested if he returned to England." Hanbury enjoyed the surprise on Dougal's face. "But there's no time for that now. Here—you'd better have these. Forty-seven Herbert Avenue, Muswell Hill. Near the golf course, I believe."

He handed Dougal two keys, a Yale and a Chubb.

"But that's miles away," Dougal said. "How did you get them?"

"Eh? Oh, Victoria had a set. Don't worry—it's all perfectly aboveboard."

"Is it? So what do I say if a neighbour calls the police?"

"That Victoria asked you to fetch her something. Anything will do—a book, perhaps. She'll back you up and so will I. But I hope it won't come to that. How have you got on today?"

Dougal shrugged. "I'd like to talk to A. J. McQuarm. No one admits to knowing a thing about him, even his gender. Something else came up. Nicholas Finwood—Olivia's twin brother. Must have been born about three years ago."

"But where is he now?"

"Apparently he's dead. I think we should find out when and why. Can you have him traced?"

"Is it relevant?"

"I don't know what's relevant and what isn't," Dougal said bitterly. "That's the trouble with this case. Everywhere you look there's a new line of enquiry. By this time you'd expect the frame to be narrowing, but it just keeps getting wider."

"This evening," Hanbury said, "we must have a long chat about it. Now you get up to Muswell Hill. I must buy an umbrella. Then I'll just pop down to Bond Street. I want to see if I can find a little something for Victoria in Asprey's."

For the fifth time Edgar Timworth picked up the phone and dialled the familiar number.

He counted the rings. After ten he was sure they must all be out. This morning he had tried the operator, who had assured him that there wasn't a fault on the line.

After the twentieth ring he put down the receiver and rested his head on his hands. In front of him on the desk was the cover proof for *Empire of Flesh and Blood.* He wished he had never seen the bloody book.

Suddenly the phone began to ring. He grabbed it, hoping against hope.

"Ed? This is Josephine Jones. I'm just ringing to prod your memory about the outline for the new McQuarm. Graham was asking about it this morning. Any news?"

The first of the unwelcome surprises that 47 Herbert Avenue had to offer was the cat.

The animal was lurking just inside the door. Dougal was ill-prepared for it. He was exhausted after the long, steep climb up Herbert Avenue from Colney Hatch Lane, where he had left the taxi in the interests of discretion. Muswell Hill was exactly what it said. You tended to forget that London, like everywhere else, had a physical geography beneath its roads and buildings. Golders Green was no longer particularly green, and Dougal had never noticed a valley in Maida Vale (maybe they had filled it in); but the hills remained, silent witnesses of a world that was older than the city above it, a world that would endure when the city was gone.

The cat was a grey, long-haired Persian. A bell hung from the flea collar round its neck. It was starved of company. Dougal pulled on a pair of disposable plastic gloves and bent to stroke it. This was the third cat in the case: the jade cat that Finwood gave Yarpole; Heliogabalus, the black and white tom in Halcombe; and now this infinitely superior specimen in Finwood's house. He found a disc on the cat's collar: MY NAME IS CLARA. IF I AM LOST, MY OWNER WILL REWARD YOU FOR MY SAFE RETURN. Underneath was a phone number.

Shit, Dougal thought. If the cat's here, someone must be coming in to feed it.

He pushed Clara away and set off towards the back of the house. Sitting room on the left, stairs on the right and a small dining room at the end of the hall. Through the dining room was the kitchen.

A tray of cat litter was standing on a sheet of newspaper under the table. Near it were bowls of food, milk and water. Clara followed him in and, despairing of attracting his attention, stuck her head in the bowl of food.

The signs were good. The cat litter was fresh. The bowls were almost full and the milk hadn't begun to separate. Unless Clara was a very small eater indeed, it was safe to assume that whoever was looking after her had called within the last few hours. In which case he or she was unlikely to call again while Dougal was here. *He or she:* the phrase reminded him of McQuarm. Clara abandoned the food and snaked round his legs.

Mewing piteously, the cat followed him from room to room as he made the preliminary survey. The house was late Victorian and detached. To his surprise Dougal rather liked it. The basement, which Finwood had turned into a utility room and wine cellar, was smaller than the floors above because the house had been built on a slope near the brow of the hill. On the ground floor the rooms were small but they had their original fireplaces, windows and mouldings. Upstairs were three bedrooms, one of which Finwood had used as a study. It was as if the builder had used a plan for a much larger house and simply halved the dimensions, which had the paradoxical effect of making it feel like an enlarged dolls' house.

He had been expecting the place to be as chaotic as Finwood's office had been. But the house was almost suspiciously tidy. It looked and smelled as if it had been recently redecorated by professionals. Who was it who had said that Finwood kept the different parts of his life in watertight compartments? Perhaps he'd had a different set of habits for each compartment. It was almost as if 47 Herbert Avenue had been inhabited by a different person from the man who had occupied the office at Gasset and Lode.

The contents were also unexpected, in the sense that many of them were valuable. In the basement Finwood had laid down three-dozen bottles of first-growth claret. The case of Dom Perignon, still unopened, hadn't come cheap, and nor had the thirty-year-old Mac-allan upstairs. The rug in the sitting room must have cost several thousand pounds; it was Turkish, which reminded Dougal of Lesley's brother Ross. Some of the furniture was astonishingly good. Most people only saw armchairs like the pair in the sitting room in a museum; judging by the hairs on the seat of one of them, Clara made a practice of sleeping there. Over the fireplace was a small Samuel Palmer landscape.

It was the same story upstairs. In the main bedroom, which was dominated by a high brass bedstead and a nineteenth-century officer's chest, Dougal opened the wardrobe and found more hand-made shoes and two suits from Gieves & Hawkes. Finwood may have had his problems but poverty wasn't among them.

So where had the money come from? Most publishers, even relatively well-established ones, don't earn a fortune. Nothing had emerged to suggest that there was money in Finwood's family; indeed, Lesley had said that Finwood had been a "scholarship boy," and Uncle Athelstan certainly didn't smack of inherited wealth.

The study was the obvious place to look for answers. It was at the front of the house, a small room with a striped Regency wallpaper that made it feel like a luxurious cage. Clara jumped on to the chair in front of an escritoire, which was against the wall opposite the door. Bookcases the height of the windowsill ran round two of the walls. Finwood had read a lot of modern poetry and fiction; and he also owned an astonishing quantity of books about cats in all their aspects. A cheap computer, similar to the one in Timworth's office, stood on a table in the corner, with discs, printer and paper on the broad shelf above it.

Dougal tried the escritoire first. It wasn't locked. The first thing he saw when he opened the hinged flap was Finwood's passport. So the man hadn't been planning to leave the country—not under his own name, at least. It had been issued only six weeks before, and the pages were blank. And the face in the photograph was the same as the face on Victoria Yarpole's wall.

The discovery removed the faint possibility that Victoria Yarpole was somehow taking himself and Hanbury for a ride. She had certainly known Finwood. Moreover, it was now confirmed beyond all doubt that the man at Sheba's Tump, the man who had posed as Finwood and made phone calls in his name from the pub, was an imposter.

Dougal rifled the drawers and compartments. In a supposedly secret drawer in the centre he found several grams of hash, wrapped in foil and enclosed in a plastic bag. Finwood's life had yet another compartment: he was—or had been—the right age to have been a part-time hippy at university. Nothing else emerged from the bills, stationery and letters apart from confirmation of the fact that Finwood had spent a good deal of money in the last few months.

He turned his attention to the three drawers below the flap. Finwood used the top one as a dumping ground for objects that had nowhere else to go. Among the contents were a ruler, rubber-bands, scissors, a broken watch, a half-completed jumbo crossword from *The Times* and an impressive collection of *Fabulous Furry Freak Brothers* comics. On top of the comics was a strip of two passport photographs, identical to the one that Dougal had already seen. He slipped them in his pocket.

The second drawer looked more promising. He rummaged through insurance policies, mortgage accounts and receipted bills until, right at the bottom, he came across a long, brown envelope; it was unsealed and labelled *The Last Will and Testament of Oswald George Finwood.* Dougal's fingers shook slightly as he opened it. Finwood had drawn up the will himself, using a form from a stationer's—another example, perhaps, of his meanness. It was dated nearly four years earlier, before the birth of the twins, and at the top was a pencilled note: "Copy—original with Ralphson."

Finwood had appointed Timworth as executor, in consideration for which he was given a legacy of £250, and left everything else "to my wife Lesley Mary Finwood." In the event of her predeceasing him, the estate went to any children he might have. The rest of it was irrelevant—what should happen if the hypothetical children were under age at their father's death, what should happen if the hypothetical children had presented their father with hypothetical grandchildren and so on.

The real question was whether the will had been superseded by a later one. The solicitor Ralphson should know. If Finwood had left his estate elsewhere, Dougal thought, Lesley and Olivia would be legally entitled to claim a share in it; but if the existing will still stood, they would get the lot. And that would solve Olivia's educational problems at a single stroke.

He pushed the will back into its envelope. As he closed the middle drawer, his mind on the will, he was aware of a car braking on the road outside. He opened the last drawer and found a collection of manila files, their contents neatly labelled. Bank statements, income tax returns, savings accounts, stocks and shares. Here if anywhere was the explanation for Finwood's wealth.

A car door closed. Then another. Below him, and somewhere outside, was a *click*. Metal on metal, Dougal thought, and instantly he knew what it was: the latch on the front gate.

He rammed the drawer shut. *Trapped—trapped—trapped.* The word circled round his mind and he wanted to scream. Instead he scrambled to his feet and, staying close to the wall, edged from the escritoire to the window. A book, Hanbury had said, that was it; he took one at random from the bookcase as he passed. He peered down between the curtain and the window frame.

A young man in a grey suit was shutting the gate. Dougal had never seen him before. Behind him was a red Japanese car—one of those sporty little numbers that look like ersatz Porsches. Not the sort of car you'd expect to find a policeman using. The man smiled and said something inaudible to someone who was already on the path.

Clara jumped off the chair and pattered down the stairs.

TEN

JEM GLANCED ALONG THE HALL, up the sweep of the stairs and back to Lesley. He raised his eyebrows and grinned. "Very impressive," he said with an ambiguity that she guessed was intentional.

"You'll want to measure up," she said. "Where do you usually start?"

"Wherever you like, Mrs. Finwood."

He was in his early twenties, she guessed, a little city slicker with swept-back hair and a suit from Next. And so anxious to put things on a personal basis that he hadn't even mentioned his surname.

"The sitting room is on your left."

"Do you mind if I eyeball the whole property first? Just to get a feel of it."

"Go ahead. I'm going to feed the cat."

Clara followed Lesley into the kitchen, but it was love she wanted, not food. She guessed that Oz must have arranged for the woman opposite to feed the cat while he was on holiday, and presumably she had just carried on when Oz failed to return. Someone else she would have to see—Mrs. Pritchard, was it? Had anyone bothered to tell her Oz was dead? A kindly person, Lesley remembered, with five children, two of whom were adopted. The sort of woman who was always doing house-to-house collections for char-

ity. The milk and food looked fresh: she'd probably come in this
afternoon.

"New fitted kitchen, eh?" Jem said behind her. "I like the oak
panelling. Very tasty."

Everything was new. This wasn't the house she had left. It even
smelled different. Relief and anger churned inside her, each one
struggling to get the upper hand. She left Jem exclaiming over the
fireplace in the sitting room and went upstairs. If she'd had any
sense, she would have come here alone the first time. Or maybe
with Olivia, because Olivia belonged so absolutely in the present
that her company left no room for the past.

Lesley hesitated on the landing. *I'm listening for ghosts.* The door
of the smallest bedroom was slightly ajar. This was the real test.
Now she was on the threshold, she didn't want to look inside. In
Halcombe it had been easy to be brave, to tell herself that the past
had lost its power to hurt. Here in the dolls' house it was different.
Oz hadn't managed to exorcize the memories.

*Two little cots and rainbows on the wall. The wallpaper cost a fortune. I
was in too much of a hurry to hang it, to get the room finished, so some of
the rainbows always looked crooked or broken. But I was right to hurry.
Something warned me I was running out of time. Broken rainbows. The
pains started just as—*

"You got some nice stuff here," Jem shouted.

She ignored him. Clara, who had followed her upstairs, lost patience with her and sidled into the main bedroom.

*And in the morning you'd find them staring at each other through the
two sets of bars. If one was giggling or crying or hungry or silent, then so
was the other—*

"What about carpets and curtains? You leaving them?"

"Yes I am," Lesley shouted back, "and I'm open to offers for
some of the furniture."

Until one morning, only Olivia was crying—

She pushed the door open so hard that it jarred against something behind it. Suddenly, as the changes Oz had made hit her,
outrage elbowed the ghosts briefly to one side. She thought that if
he had been there, standing just inside the room and smiling in that

conceited way of his, she would have killed him for his insensitivity. How could any normal person have stayed here?

Jem was coming up the stairs. She backed away—the other business would have to wait—and turned into the main bedroom. Tears blurred her vision but automatically she registered the differences: new bed, new everything; he had removed every trace of her and the children. She took a tissue from the box by the chest of drawers and quickly wiped her eyes. Jem, who had merely poked his head into the other rooms, appeared in the doorway.

"Well, it's a nice little property. Period character, in beautiful nick. Good size, too: not too big, not too small. Flexible accommodation. You could turn the basement into a granny flat, maybe, or a room for the au pair. Even use it as an office, I suppose. Is there a garage?"

She shook her head.

"Can't be helped." He sidled towards her, the mindless professional patter oozing out of him. "At least there's plenty of on-street parking. It's a nice, safe residential location. The back garden must be very secluded. There's just one thing: it might be worth cutting the lawn before we put it on the market."

Lesley moved away from him and looked out of the window. Same old view. Oz had always hated gardening.

"What do you think we could get?" she said.

"Ah, well—difficult to say exactly. As you probably know, the market is dead at present. We're hoping for an upward curve in spring. It all depends on the interest rates. After Christmas—that's when people start thinking about moving."

"I don't want to wait that long."

Jem joined her by the window. She hated people who stood close to her. She felt menaced. His aftershave revolted her. It probably had a name like Sport or Mr. Macho.

"You got to be prepared to wait with a house like this," he said. "It's all psychology. Somewhere out there is a person who'd pay the earth for this. It's unique, see? The sort of house that people take a fancy to, and then they don't mind what they pay for it. Of course you might just get lucky—the right person could come along tomorrow. But I wouldn't bank on it."

He paused, waiting for her to agree with him. The anticipation on his face made her want to giggle. He looked just like a conjuror who has produced a rabbit out of his hat and is now waiting with ill-concealed anxiety for the applause. In this case the rabbit was an expert opinion, one of those precious snippets of professional advice which the donor hopes the recipient will value as highly as he does.

Of course he was right: you didn't have to be an estate agent to know that people buy houses with their hearts, not their heads. She'd first seen this house nearly four years earlier on a rainy November afternoon, and she'd known at once that she wanted it. And Oz had thought it would be a good investment.

"Take my advice," Jem went on confidentially, "you play a waiting game. It'd pay you to, in the long run. You'd make an extra ten or twenty K. Maybe more, if the market recovers."

He mentioned a price range that surprised her: it was more than she had dared hope for. Even if the house sold for the lowest figure, she would be able to pay off the mortgage that had once seemed so huge and still make enough to buy another house outright in Halcombe.

"I want it sold as quickly as possible," she said.

"Relocation, is it? Your husband's got a job somewhere else?"

She disliked the implied sexism in the question but let it go.

"No," she said. "My husband's just died. That's why I want to get shot of it as soon as I can."

"Oh. Sorry about that."

Flushing, he backed away from her, as though Oz's death had touched her with a contagion that she could pass to him. He was very young; and dying was still a process that happened to other people.

Lesley looked through the rain-streaked window and wondered what she would do with the contents of the house. Some of them were obviously very valuable. She heard Jem's breathing; and somewhere in the room Clara was purring. The cat was another problem. She'd have to find a home for Clara. It would be nice to get rid of Heliogabalus, too. She had had enough of cats. They reminded her of Oz.

"I'd better measure up," Jem said. "Uh—I'll start with the basement, okay?"

He blundered out of the room and down the stairs. Lesley opened her handbag and took out two carrier bags. There was work to do. She went into the room that Oz had used as a study. She took the box of tissues with her. Just as a precaution.

The tension had settled round Timworth's head. He visualized it as a steel band, which, like a medieval instrument of torture, was gradually tightening. During the afternoon, the headache grew worse and worse, far beyond the reach of the painkillers in the bathroom cupboard.

He lay in the bedroom with the curtains drawn; the darkness helped a little. The red display of the digital clock blinked at him. He disciplined himself to wait fifteen minutes between each attempt.

On the hour, at a quarter-past, at half-past and at quarter-to, he would pick up the phone and punch the last-number-redial button.

And each time the phone rang in his ear—on and on for twenty rings until he replaced the receiver.

"Mr. Hanbury? Your call to Istanbul is through. Line three."

"Thank you, Cynthia." Hanbury cleared his throat and opened the phrasebook. "Hello?" he said loudly. "Is that the RK Transcaucasian Export Company?"

He was answered by a squeak whose origin might have been either human or electronic. He raised his voice and repeated the question.

Another squeak—this time definitely from a human source. Hanbury ran his finger down the second page of the phrasebook. Number 17 should fit the bill.

"Burada İngilizce," he said carefully, *"bilen kimse var mi?"*

"What?"

"I said, does anyone speak English?"

"Of course I do," said a man with a strong Glaswegian accent. "I'm a Scot, aren't I?"

"I'm trying to get in touch with Mr. Ross Kanaird."

"Business or personal is it?"

"Ah—personal. In a manner of speaking."

"Well, in a manner of speaking he's not available just now."

"It's rather urgent," Hanbury said.

"He's on holiday."

"Who am I speaking to?"

"I could take a message," the Scot offered.

"Do you know where he's gone?"

"Could be anywhere. And I don't know when he'll be back, either. Do you want to leave a message or not?"

"I don't think I will, thank you." Hanbury wondered if the Scot and Kanaird were one and the same person. "I'll try his mother first, and one or two other people." He gave the Scot a couple of seconds to stop stonewalling and admit either that he was Kanaird or that he knew where Kanaird was. "If that fails, I'll be in touch again."

He broke the connection. For a moment he stared at the grey and swirling waters of the river below. The telephone call had been a gamble. At present there was no way of knowing whether he had won or lost. If only Winston Yarpole would see sense and stop being so insular in his thinking. If Custodemus were truly global in its operations, this line of enquiry could have been switched over to the Turkish office.

One day, Hanbury promised himself, one day.

It was a tight fit under the bed, so tight that he wondered whether he would ever be able to get out.

The base of the metal frame that supported the springs dug into Dougal's chest. Once, while they were talking a few feet away from him, he was gripped by an almost irresistible urge to cough. He fought it by swallowing constantly, trying to generate saliva in his mouth, and by thinking of running water and honey and glasses of beer.

The book he had brought with him in his panic was a battered paperback copy of *Fathers and Sons*. While Lesley and the man were still downstairs he looked at the flyleaf. The book had once belonged to Ross Kanaird.

The twin constraints of fear and the metal frame made it difficult to control his breathing. To him it sounded ragged and loud. On either side of the bed the duvet hung down almost to the floor. He was more in danger of their hearing him than seeing him.

Clara nosed aside the bottom of the duvet and slipped underneath. She seemed totally unsurprised to find a human being under the bed. Her only discernable reaction was pleasurable anticipation. Purring loudly, she crept up the length of his body until she reached the head. She butted his cheek with her nose. In desperation he brought his hand up and tickled her under the chin.

At that moment Lesley came into the room, and the man soon followed. An estate agent; and Lesley wanted a quick sale. Soon, Dougal was convinced, one of them would lift up the duvet to discover what was driving Clara to such a peak of ecstasy. He stopped scratching her chin and she let out an aggrieved miaow. Quickly he started again, on the assumption that purring was less likely to attract their attention than miaowing.

Eventually they left him alone with Clara. Lesley was in Finwood's study. He heard her opening the drawers of the escritoire and moving about. The estate agent was all over the place. Once he returned to the bedroom. A steel tape measure whirred and clicked. Clara stopped purring and abandoned Dougal to investigate.

"Hello, kitty. Nice kitty," said the estate agent; and he must have succumbed to her advances because Clara's purr, as regular as the hum of a well-oiled sewing machine, began again.

Later, footsteps went down the stairs. Later still, the estate agent called up: "All finished now." There were more footsteps, lighter than the first set, on the stairs: Lesley going to join him in the hall. Voices murmured. A click as the front door opened; a bang as it closed. Dougal sighed and allowed himself a small, dry cough. He heard, or thought he heard, the click of the gate. A car door slammed. The pseudo-Porsche's engine fired with a wholly unnecessary roar.

Dougal began to wriggle sideways into the daylight. The frame of the bedstead pressed into him, unwilling to let him go. His muscles were stiff, his throat was dry and he realized that he was covered with chilly sweat. It didn't matter.

Oh God . . . Footsteps were coming up the stairs.

Frantically he wriggled back. Lesley was still here. She went into the study. The minutes crawled by, punctuated by the rustle of paper from the next room. At least Clara had left him alone. Dougal's panic gave way to a dull and deep depression. Sooner or later he would give himself away; sooner or later she would find him. He wished he had made his presence known as soon as she had come into the house. His excuse—the book for Yarpole—was a thin one but at least it had made some sort of sense. It was too late for that now: nothing he could do or say could prevent Lesley from thinking him both foolish and criminal. He would have given anything to have been able to have a drink of water and use the lavatory.

At one point Lesley came into the bedroom. She was talking to herself, as people often do when they believe that they are alone; but her voice was too low for him to catch what she was saying. He heard her opening the door of the wardrobe and, later, the drawers in the chest. Packing up Oz's clothes? No—there wasn't time for that. More probably she was looking for something.

The doorbell rang.

Let it be a taxi, Dougal prayed. She had come in the estate agent's car. Lesley went downstairs. In a moment there were voices in the hall. Feet pounded up the stairs.

"Where's the cat, Mummy? Where's the cat?"

"She's not going to come out if you make that sort of noise," Lesley said. "Now just calm down, will you?"

"What are you going to do with that animal?" It was Mrs. Kanaird's dry, precise voice. "We haven't room for two."

"I don't know. Sell it, perhaps. It's a thoroughbred or whatever they call them. I found its pedigree in there."

By now they were all on the landing.

"Was it Daddy's cat?" Olivia said. "Can I have it?"

"No," Lesley snapped; and Olivia pretended to cry.

"I suppose we'll have to take it with us," Mrs. Kanaird said. "Just for the time being, I mean. We can't very well leave it here."

"How do we find it?" Olivia asked.

"Rattle a fork against a tin: that'll bring it out."

"The cat basket's in the basement," Lesley said. "I've filled a few bags, Mum. The rest can wait."

"What are you taking?"

"Papers mainly. Ed and the solicitor need to go through them."

"Mummy, have I been here before?"

"Yes," Lesley said. "A long time ago."

"Before I was born?"

"No, after that. Can you carry that bag downstairs? *Carefully.*"

"Oz really made some changes." By the sound of her Mrs. Kanaird was in the bedroom. "No expense spared." She lowered her voice. "And just for himself and that wretched animal."

"He loved cats," Lesley said. "You've got to give him that."

"He's welcome to them."

They went up and down the stairs, stockpiling things in the hall. Clara was captured. Olivia ran about, getting in the others' way. No one came into the bedroom.

"I've left Henry upstairs," Olivia shrieked.

"Well, go and get him. Granny and I are going to load the car."

Olivia was not a graceful child. She thundered up the stairs and burst into the bedroom. Dougal listened to her heavy breathing. It came closer and closer.

Without warning a corner of the duvet was tweaked aside. Olivia lay on her front, holding her doll by its long, fair hair and looking straight at Dougal. It was dark under the bed, but not that dark; he knew that she must have seen him. Her face showed interest, not surprise. There was an outside chance that she hadn't recognized him. Not yet.

"Mummy! There's a man under the bed!"

Dougal shut his eyes, the last resort of those who can no longer cope with life.

"What did you say?" Lesley shouted.

"I'm not a man," Dougal whispered. "I'm a tiger."

"Mummy, there's a tiger under the bed. It's smiling at me."

"Yes, dear. Come along now. We're going."

ELEVEN

"IS EVERYTHING to your satisfaction, Mr. Hanbury?"

"Almost perfect." Hanbury paused, enjoying the flicker of anxiety in the little man's eyes. Julio held himself rigidly, like a dog waiting on tenterhooks for his master's command. It was very satisfactory indeed. "The yolks," Hanbury went on, "are just a trifle too well-done for my taste."

"But they're just right for mine," Dougal said.

Julio ignored the interruption. "I shall speak to her. I shall have words."

"Do remember to congratulate her on the bacon," Hanbury said. "Could we have some more coffee?"

"I'm not impressed," Dougal said when Julio had gone. "Just disgusted."

"You've got to keep these people up to the mark," Hanbury said, marvelling at Dougal's failure to grasp such a fundamental imperative of social interaction. "Otherwise they get slack. Really, this place is quite a find. They do a very reasonable breakfast, and it's only a stone's throw from the office."

"Are you planning to tell me why we've come here?"

"Because I thought you'd be interested." Hanbury lowered his voice. "Julio used to be in partnership with Ross Kanaird. He was lucky not to end up in jail."

"How do you know that?"

How typical of William, Hanbury thought, with a glow of proprietorial pride: the scholar in him insists on checking his sources.

Aloud he said, "As Kanaird lives abroad, I thought I might run his name through the Customs and Excise computer. And up came details of an investigation they did. Inconclusive—it didn't lead to prosecution, partly because of lack of evidence and partly because our friend Ross moved out of their jurisdiction. When I turned up yesterday and asked about Ross, Julio immediately assumed I was a VAT investigation officer. That's why we're being pampered."

For a moment they ate in silence. Hanbury noted, with approval, that Dougal did not enquire about the nature of the connection between Custodemus and HM Customs and Excise. The connection, of course, was yet another illustration of one of the simpler facts about human nature: that what counts is not so much what you know as whom you know—or rather whom you have on your payroll.

Julio brought them a fresh pot of coffee. He wanted to talk, or perhaps to be reassured, but Hanbury shooed him away. The cafe was in a sidestreet off Fetter Lane. On the walls were framed views of Capri and Vesuvius, their colours bleached by the sun. It was still early—not yet eight o'clock—but already a steady flow of customers poured in and out; some bought takeaway cups of tea and bacon rolls; others munched steadily behind newspapers at the formica-topped tables. There was little conversation. People came here solely to eat, to prepare themselves for the transition from home to work. Julio had built up an efficient little operation, Hanbury thought; probably it was entirely legitimate, unlike the capital that had funded it. As he mopped up the last of his egg yolk with a piece of roll, he wondered how Julio's wife, who was presumably as Italian as her husband, had mastered the intricacies of the English breakfast.

"Ross and Julio seem to have gone about it in quite an intelligent way," Hanbury said to Dougal. "They had at least three schemes operating, and literally scores of false companies, here and abroad. One scheme involved illegally importing wholesale goods and then selling them with the full fifteen-percent VAT added to the price—

which of course they pocketed. Anything with a fixed retail price would do—from gold to soft drinks. Some of the export companies claimed VAT rebates for goods which didn't exist. They also had a rather clever system for generating false invoices for non-existent goods that were sold from company to company to company: at each transaction they reclaimed a little VAT; and over the whole series they reclaimed a small fortune."

"Would Ross actually be arrested if he came back?"

Hanbury shrugged. "They'd certainly want to talk to him. His passport's been flagged. They think he was the brains behind it, you see; he trained as an accountant. I understand that they've less evidence against Julio. But enough to make them look very carefully at his returns."

Dougal aligned his knife and fork on the empty plate. "What about Mrs. Kanaird?"

"We didn't have much luck there. I sent a man down to dig around. She's a widow—her husband was a salesman for an engineering firm; spent a lot of time abroad; died young and left her a widow's pension that doesn't amount to much. She used to be a classics teacher at Halcombe Grammar School. She stayed on when they turned comprehensive but took early retirement. Small, shrinking income. She doesn't even own her house—it's on a lease that's coming up for renewal in five years' time. No debts, which isn't significant: that generation doesn't like credit."

"Did you get anywhere with Lesley?"

Hanbury glanced at him, wondering if he had imagined the alteration in Dougal's tone. *That* would be an unwelcome complication. He'd seen Lesley only once, at the funeral and the reception on Monday. An attractive woman, certainly, but not in the same class as Celia Prentisse, who was very nearly beautiful—and, of course, very much richer. He hoped that William wasn't on the brink of doing something foolish.

"My—ah—researchers didn't find much about her. Local schools, then Essex University. Drifted into teaching like her mother but in the private sector, and then drifted out as soon as she married Finwood. Soon after that, they had the twins. The boy,

Nicholas, died when he was just over six months old. It was one of those cot deaths—Sudden Infant Death Syndrome, is it? Probably boils down to parental negligence, wouldn't you think?"

"No," Dougal said, "I wouldn't."

Hanbury belatedly realized that Dougal was a parent and that Eleanor wasn't much older than six months. "Of course, if you're right about the will," he said quickly, "Lesley stands to gain more than anyone from Finwood's death—financially, that is. What do you think it adds up to?"

"I don't know." Dougal began to roll a cigarette. "It's McQuarm that worries me."

"They all knew one another—Ross, Finwood and Timworth. Timworth and Ross went to the same school. Finwood and Timworth went to the same university. And both of them wanted to marry Ross's sister."

"A conspiracy? And the other two ganged up on Ross? It doesn't explain the switch of identity." Dougal paused to lick the cigarette paper. "There are too many people and too many motives. For example, Josephine Jones hated Oz, and now he's dead she's got his job."

"Victoria is very keen to see some results," Hanbury said.

"In that case we have to go down to Halcombe and have a chat with Lesley and Mrs. Kanaird. I don't see what else we can do."

"Is this—ah—wise, William? I thought we agreed it would be dangerous to alert them prematurely."

"They're the only people who can sort out the identity of the body. We've gone as far as we can go in other directions. The only alternative is to go to the police."

"Don't be childish," Hanbury snapped. He struggled to retain his temper. "Be reasonable, William. We've been into all this. The police mean publicity. If Victoria's father even begins to suspect she was having an affair with Finwood, things are going to become very awkward indeed. For all of us."

"Have you a better idea?"

"All right." Hanbury hated the feeling that he was facing the unknown. For different reasons, Victoria and William were prodding him forward. He lit a cigarette and dwelled briefly on the unthinkable: what Yarpole could do if he discovered that Hanbury had been doing this sort of favour for his daughter. The disclosure would certainly destroy his hopes of eventually controlling Custodemus; Yarpole would use his majority shareholding to push Hanbury out of an active role in the company. Almost equally unpleasant was the prospect of what Victoria might do if she discovered that the corpse at Sheba's Tump had not belonged to Finwood, and that he, Hanbury, had been well aware of this for some time. Almost: but not quite. He wondered if there might be something to be said for making a relatively clean breast of the whole matter to Winston Yarpole.

"Well?" Dougal said.

"You'd better go to Halcombe this morning," Hanbury said. "But handle it very carefully. Just turn up and wave that photograph of Finwood under their noses. Don't be too—ah—threatening. If I were you, I'd—"

"We can talk about how we handle it on the way."

"Eh?"

"I think we should do this together."

"Quite impossible. I've got a very busy morning ahead."

Dougal smiled. Smoke dribbled out of his nostrils. "I'm not going alone."

Timworth put down the phone and flicked through the morning's post.

Two parcels from aspiring authors whose talents did not match their aspirations, and probably never would; they were always sending him manuscripts and he wasn't sufficiently ruthless to tell them to stop. Three bills. Six circulars. A cheque from Gasset and Lode. And one letter in a long, white envelope.

He opened the envelope last of all. His mind was still taken up with Lesley—or, rather, with Lesley's absence. The envelope contained four sheets of A4 paper. The first sheet was dated yesterday. There was no address.

```
Dear Mr. Timworth
I enclose a brief outline for a possible follow-up to
EMPIRE OF FLESH AND BLOOD. It has the provisional
title of THE CHILD OF RUSSIA. I hope you like it. I
estimate it would take me about a year and a half to
complete, assuming that Gasset and Lode are willing to
commission it on terms that are agreeable to us both. I
imagine they will want roughly the same length as last
time i.e., about 180,000 words.
   I am aware, of course, that the tragic death of Mr.
Finwood must necessarily change the nature of our
relationship. I expect you have many questions you
would like to ask me. As you know, I have always
insisted on anonymity, and I hope you will not mind if
I retain that anonymity a little longer. I shall be in
touch again when you have had Gasset and Lode's
response.
```

The signature was an illegible squiggle. Underneath was printed "A. J. McQuarm."

When the shock had subsided, Timworth's first thought was that this must be some sort of hoax on the part, perhaps, of someone at Gasset and Lode. He skimmed through the outline. The new plot had the same blend of sex, sensation and exotic locations as *Empire of Flesh and Blood,* perhaps in a more concentrated form; and if anything the storyline was even more implausible. The real thing or a skilful pastiche?

Timworth rubbed his forehead. He'd taken a couple of Sodium Amytal last night, and his mind was still fogged with sleep. No, it couldn't be a hoax, or at least not a harmless one, because the writer of the letter quite obviously knew a good deal about "the nature of our relationship."

Somewhere out there—Timworth grabbed the envelope and looked at the postmark—somewhere in *London,* A. J. McQuarm was panting to begin the next schlockbuster.

The thought terrified him.

When the doorbell rang, Mrs. Kanaird was unpacking in her bed-room. The window overlooked the garden and as she unpacked she was also keeping an eye on Lesley's bonfire, which was still smouldering near the wall at the bottom. It was almost out but you could never tell with bonfires.

Clara and Hell tried to trip her on the stairs.

Mrs. Kanaird surprised and shocked herself: "Won't you bugger off?" she screamed.

She aimed a kick at Clara, who easily avoided it. Mrs. Kanaird clung to the banisters. Yesterday had been exhausting, and she never slept well in strange beds. She found it difficult to share Lesley's optimism. Worst of all, beneath the layers of tiredness and worry was the bedrock of grief. Grief like that, she knew from experience, was something you could never lose. As time went by, it became easier to forget, sometimes for quite long periods. But it was always there, waiting with dreadful patience for the unguarded moment and the unexpected jolt from your memory.

Two men were waiting outside on the pavement. One was William Dougal. The other was an older man whom she had seen beside Victoria Yarpole at the funeral on Monday. Slightly overweight and very well-dressed, he looked like one of those character actors who turn up time and time again in television sitcoms about middle-class life. Automatically she tried to close the door.

The older man's umbrella shot out. The tip brushed against the jamb and thudded on to the doormat inside.

"Do go away," Mrs. Kanaird said. "We've only just got back and I'm very tired." The words were petulant and, worse still, irrelevant. She tightened her grip on the doorknob and said, "I must ask you to leave."

"We'd just like to ask you one question," Dougal said. "I'm sorry to butt in like this."

"If you were really sorry," she said tartly, "you wouldn't do it. Please remove the umbrella."

"This is my colleague, James Hanbury."

"I don't care who he is. I've got nothing to say to you. If you don't leave I shall call the police."

"I wouldn't advise that," said the man called Hanbury. "Not yet, at least. If I were you, I'd hear the question first."

"If you have anything to say to me, you can talk to my solicitor."

Dougal cleared his throat. "Is Mrs. Finwood in? This concerns her as well. More so, in a way."

Mrs. Kanaird's hand slipped from the door. She wondered if he'd said that intentionally, if he'd calculated the effect it would have on her. There was no reason why he shouldn't know that the urge to protect is the greatest weakness of love, as well as its greatest strength.

"She's out," Mrs. Kanaird heard herself saying. "I don't know when she'll be back."

"It would be better to go inside," Dougal said; and she hated the gentleness in his voice because it showed that he knew precisely what he was doing.

She retreated into the hall, past Lesley's case, Olivia's toys and the bags they had brought from Oz's house. The Samuel Palmer was there, its face turned to the wall.

"A lovely painting." Dougal actually patted the frame as he passed. "I envy you that."

She looked at him sharply, her mind racing through the implications of that apparently innocuous remark. In the sitting room the phone began to ring. It was a welcome diversion. She ran into the room, reaching the phone on the third ring.

"Louisa? It's Ed. Is Lesley there?"

"No, she's out."

"Where have you been? I've been trying to get hold of you since yesterday morning."

"We were up in town," Mrs. Kanaird said, puzzled. She had assumed that Lesley would have told Timworth that she was going to Oz's house. "We spent the night with some friends of Lesley's. I thought—"

"When will she be back?"

"I don't know exactly. It shouldn't be long."

"Would you ask her to ring me as soon as she gets in? It's urgent."

"All right. Can I take a message?"

"No, you can't," he said with a bluntness that was most unlike him. "I must go."

He put down the phone without saying goodbye. She realized that Dougal was standing just behind her. Hanbury had wandered across to the window, where he was examining the photographs that were ranged along the sill. Mrs. Kanaird wished she had taken her visitors into the kitchen.

Dougal didn't bother to disguise the fact that he had been eavesdropping. "Timworth is in a bit of state by the sound of him," he said. "He was all right when I saw him yesterday."

She frowned, trying to work out what he was driving at. He'd spoken as if Edgar was somehow involved, which was nonsense. Edgar was where he always was: on the sidelines.

Hanbury put down the photograph of Nick and Olivia. Suddenly Mrs. Kanaird remembered Nick's tiny coffin, and how Lesley had stood with dry eyes by the grave, and, after the funeral, how Lesley had clung to Olivia and wept.

"Well, what do you want to ask?" she said harshly.

Dougal took out his wallet and extracted a strip of passport photographs. "This is Oz Finwood," he said. "But it's not the man I found at Sheba's Tump."

"Don't be absurd," Mrs. Kanaird said.

"Do you want to explain? Or shall we go to the police?"

"If I went to bed in my Wellies," Olivia said, "the spiders couldn't get me."

Lesley glanced in the rear-view mirror. "If you went to bed in your Wellies, darling, I'd be very, *very* cross."

She indicated left and hauled on the wheel. Her mother's old Cortina estate was the devil to drive—the steering was heavy, second gear tended to slip into neutral at the slightest provocation and you never knew how fast you were going because the speedometer no longer worked. The car rolled down the approach road to the council dump and slid under the boom. On the other side were ten covered skips the size of caravans. Lesley joined the queue of cars that were waiting to discharge their contents.

"Mummy," Olivia said. "Can I have a bicycle?"

"It's 'may I,' not 'can I.' "

"May I? Please?"

"Yes, dear. I'll buy you one this afternoon."

The surprise on Olivia's face made Lesley burst out laughing. Everything was going to be all right. The funeral was over. She now knew almost exactly what the financial position was. It was as though she had emerged from a long, dark tunnel into the daylight. The only possible problem was Ed, but he could be guaranteed to fall over himself in his eagerness to find a solution for it. At last she could allow herself to believe in happy endings.

"A red one?" Olivia asked.

"If we can find one."

"With lights and a bell?" Having recovered from the shock, Olivia was determined to make the most of her mother's generosity. "Can it have a basket for my private papers?"

"I don't know, love. We'll go and see what Haldane's have got."

Haldane's was the garage near the by-pass. While they were there, Lesley thought, she would have a look at the cars—new as well as second-hand. The bank would give her a loan on the strength of a letter from the solicitor. The world was crowded with new possibilities.

A elderly man in blue overalls rapped on the window: "Just those sacks, is it?"

Lesley nodded. Apart from herself, Olivia and the car itself, there was nothing else it could have been.

"Third skip on the right, okay?"

The dustmen would have taken the three bags on Monday but it was safer to get rid of them this way. Lesley raised the tailgate.

"Don't move," she ordered Olivia.

She staggered over to the skip with the sacks, one at a time. As she dropped each one in, her happiness increased. In her mind she saw a balloon gaining height as, one by one, the sacks of ballast were thrown overboard. *It's going to be all right.* When she came back the second time she found Olivia had wriggled out of her child-seat and climbed into the back of the car.

"It feels like clothes and things in that one," Olivia said, her hands tugging at the knot at the top of the bag. "Why don't we give them to Mrs. Portnum like we usually do?"

Lesley snatched the bag away from her. "Because she wouldn't want them, that's why. They're very dirty. And if you want that bike, you'd better get back in your seat."

She carried the last sack to the skip. It was much lighter than the other two. Through the thin material of the plastic she felt the outlines of some of the objects inside. The skip was already half-full of rubbish—mainly pruned branches and rusting household appliances. She held open the flap with one hand and tossed in the bag with the other. She threw it as high as she could. It landed on top of the pile and rolled out of sight. She laughed aloud.

"Someone's feeling cheerful this morning," said the man in the blue overalls. "Won the pools, have we?"

"Not quite," Lesley said, grinning back at him. "But it's a nice day. How's business?"

"Brisk, you could say." He examined her figure in the discreet, almost decorous way that older men sometimes manage after a lifetime of practice; she was flattered, not offended. "A lot of people clear out stuff at the end of the summer. It's a busy time of year."

Lesley waved at the row of green skips. "What do they *do* with it all?"

"They chuck it in a great big hole and cover it with topsoil: that's what they do. Leave it for the next generation to worry about."

He chuckled and moved away to deal with the next carload. Lesley walked slowly back to the Cortina. It was good to be outside in the sun, even in the middle of the council tip.

"Where are we going now?" Olivia wanted to know.

"Shopping. We need some food. And I tell you what: let's buy Granny a present."

"I don't know where to begin," Mrs. Kanaird said. "Or even if I should."

In their way the two men had been kind to her. Hanbury, clucking gently, had settled her in a chair and pushed her head between her knees until the faintness subsided. Dougal fetched her some water. Heliogabalus climbed on to her lap. She pushed him off.

"It would be better to tell us," Dougal said. "If you do, it may not go any further. But if you don't—"

"I'm afraid our client will insist on calling in the police," Hanbury interrupted. "They'll have to listen to her. And you know what the police are like: once they start, they're very hard to stop. But if she learns the full story from us—together with any extenuating circumstances—she may—ah—decide not to proceed any further. She's not a vengeful woman."

"I don't know what to do for the best," Mrs. Kanaird said.

"When I got the water," Dougal said, "I saw you've been having a bonfire. And you've had the flagstones laid. Is that where you put Finwood? Under the hardcore in the old pond?"

TWELVE

IT HAD BEGUN ON FRIDAY, not Saturday. Mrs. Kanaird closed her eyes. There was no need to make a conscious effort to remember. She had lived with this memory continuously for what seemed like years.

Yes, it had started on the Friday, the day before Oz died and the day she had met Mrs. Portnum in the butcher's. The sun shone out of a cloudless sky, and a late crop of tourists had sprouted in St. Stephen's churchyard. Mrs. Kanaird hurried home from the shops, sweating in the heat. The chicken she had bought for the weekend bounced against her leg. She had left a cake in the oven, and Mrs. Portnum had made her late.

As soon as she opened the front door, she knew that the house was not as she had left it. The others were in Gloucester for the afternoon; Lesley was shopping and Olivia would be pretending to be a baby elephant or a growing tree at her dancing class; they wouldn't be back until five o'clock. The hall smelled of cigarettes.

"Hello?" she called, fighting back her fear. "Is anyone there?"

In the kitchen the cake had been turned out of its tin and left to cool on the grid from the grill pan. The gin bottle, now empty, had moved from the cupboard to the table. The back door was standing open. Mrs. Kanaird looked through the window into the garden.

And there he was, just beyond the stack of paving stones and the heap of rubble. Relief flooded over her. He was sitting in the least uncomfortable deckchair with his back to the house. She knew who it was immediately—though all she could see of him was the back of his head, which was partly covered by her husband's gardening hat, and a pair of hairy forearms with a newspaper stretched between them.

She went outside. The first thing she noticed was that he had shaved off his beard, which made him look much younger. Heliogabalus was curled up on his lap.

"Darling, how nice to see you," she said, pushing aside all the unwelcome qualifications. "How are you?"

Ross threw down *The Independent* and stood up. Hell tumbled on to the grass with a squawk of protest. Ross hugged her; as a child he had needed a lot of cuddles and kisses, far more than Lesley ever had. Mrs. Kanaird smelled the gin and tobacco on his breath and felt the stubble on his cheek; but none of those things mattered.

"You might have phoned," she said. "What are you doing here? Is it—well, *safe* to come here?"

Still holding her, he said, "Now, don't fuss, Mum. Sit down. I'll get another chair."

"Thank you for taking the cake out," she said. She liked being able to praise Ross. "It was very thoughtful."

"The least I could do."

He fetched a chair from the porch and sat down beside her. She thought he looked ill, and that living in a hot country hadn't done much to reduce his usual pallor.

"I wanted to surprise you," he said. "Besides, I wasn't sure I could make it."

That was vintage Ross, of course—the desire never to be pinned down to a timetable, never to anticipate the future.

"When did you get here?"

"About half an hour ago."

"Did you park at the back? I didn't notice a car."

"No—I came by train." He picked up his glass. "Cheers. I'm afraid I finished the gin. I'll buy you some more."

She doubted that. *"Is* it safe for you to come home?"

"Well, let's say it's better that the news doesn't get around. I flew to Dublin and came across by the boat train."

"But, darling, everyone knows you round here. Even without the beard—"

"Don't fuss. I won't go out. In a night or two I'll be gone."

"But Olivia will see you. And Oz is coming to lunch tomorrow."

"Oz? I thought he was right off the menu."

"He is. But Lesley wants a talk with him about the divorce. About Olivia's future, really."

"She'll have to fight for every penny," Ross said. "Look, I won't get in the way. Is anyone in my room?"

She shook her head.

"Well, then. I can lurk up there like Mrs. Rochester while Oz is on the premises. We'll think of something to tell Olivia. Just pretend I'm a friend or something. You worry too much."

She shied away from the irritation in his voice. "So why did you come?"

"To see my nearest and dearest, of course."

He wanted money, she guessed; he usually did. There wasn't much left to give him—only the brooch that had belonged to her mother-in-law. The brooch—a solitaire set in an oval of smaller stones—had been valued for insurance at six thousand pounds, and that was four years ago. Mrs. Kanaird had been keeping it for a rainy day: to help with Olivia's education, perhaps; or to use as a deposit for a flat when the lease ran out on this house.

"How's the business going?" she asked.

"Not too well." Ross rummaged in his jacket, which was lying on the grass. He took his time over lighting a cigarette. "Actually, I've had a run of bad luck. Credit's been a bit of a problem." He glanced at her, his eyes narrowing to bright blue slits. "We'll talk about it later."

"As you like, dear." Mrs. Kanaird knew better than to press him. "I'll put the kettle on."

She did more than that. She went upstairs and made the bed in Ross's room, which was at the back of the house on the top floor. On the way down she slipped into her own bedroom. The jewel box was at the back of the centre drawer of the dressing table. To her relief, the little leather case that held the brooch was still inside. The case was heavy in her hand.

Her relief at finding it was tinged with guilt, for having suspected that it might not be there, and also with sorrow, because the suspicion had been well-grounded in experience. She returned the box to the drawer. Just for a moment she opened the case. The big diamond sparkled like a broken rainbow in the light from the window.

Mrs. Kanaird shrugged. They could all do with few pots of gold, but you didn't find those at the ends of broken rainbows. Rainbows reminded her of the wallpaper in the twins' bedroom at Muswell Hill. Her eyes filled with tears, partly for Nick and Ross but mostly for herself. She closed the case and, standing on tiptoe, tucked it on top of the wardrobe. Over the weekend she would have to make a decision. She had no intention of allowing Ross to make it for her.

At first the weekend went more smoothly that Mrs. Kanaird had dared hope.

Ross and Lesley had never been close. They squabbled almost continuously through childhood. Ross, the elder by four years, had the advantage of being able to resort to violence. Lesley made up for her lack of muscle by being more vindictive; she had always been the cleverer of the two, and she had been good at telling long, circumstantial lies that placed her in the right and Ross in the wrong. Children, Mrs. Kanaird often thought, are basically little beasts whose natural habitat is the jungle.

As adults, her own children had settled into a truce, largely because they met only occasionally and their interests rarely conflicted. The truce continued when Lesley and Olivia returned from Gloucester and found Ross with a new bottle of gin in the garden. This surprised Mrs. Kanaird because Lesley must have known why Ross had come home.

Olivia hadn't met Ross since she was a baby. She took one look at him and, struck by shyness, suddenly developed an intense interest in the pile of paving stones.

"This is David," Mrs. Kanaird said with a warning glance at Lesley. "He's a cousin from abroad."

"Hello, David." Lesley kissed him on the cheek. "This *is* a surprise. Are you staying long?"

Curiously enough, Ross and Olivia got on very well. While she ate her tea, he told her stories about living with tigers in India, where he had never been, and treated her as though she were an adult; for Olivia this had all the charm of novelty and she responded by behaving unusually well for the rest of Friday evening.

Olivia was put to bed and the adults settled down to supper. It was a friendly affair, with the conversation never straying towards dangerous topics. Afterwards, Ross washed up and Lesley dried. Mrs. Kanaird, who was on the move between the kitchen and the sitting room, overheard snatches of what they were saying.

"I was sorry to hear about Nick," Ross said. "Really I was. It must have been bloody awful for you."

"It wasn't much fun," Lesley said. "And Oz made it worse."

"I always said he was a shit. Don't tell him I'm back, will you?"

"Why not?"

"You know what he's like." Turning to put a plate on the rack, Ross saw Mrs. Kanaird in the doorway. "Nice kid, Olivia," he said. "Does she go to school yet?"

Saturday had been warm but the sky was overcast—promising rain that didn't arrive until Sunday.

Lesley had arranged for Olivia to spend most of the day with friends. The friends knew the circumstances and would keep Olivia with them until Oz had left. No one had told Olivia that Oz was coming; nevertheless she knew. The subject surfaced without warning at breakfast.

Olivia, who was picking shreds of straw from one of the mats, said, "Is Oz my *daddy?*"

If she'd spoken in Latin, Mrs. Kanaird thought, she'd have used *num,* the interrogative conjunction for a question that expects a negative answer.

"Of course he is," Lesley said. "Why don't you stop pulling that mat apart and finish your toast?"

Olivia obeyed her. Mrs. Kanaird wished she had continued to ask questions. Instead, she was unusually silent while she finished her meal; she hardly squirmed at all, and none of her breakfast ended up on the floor. It was unnerving. When it was time to leave, however, Olivia threw a heavy-duty tantrum; and Lesley had to drag her, kicking and screaming, out of the house, down the garden and through the gate into the lane.

Ross came down in time to witness their departure. He was still in his pyjamas. "What's up with her?"

"She knows that Oz is coming. The kettle's hot if you want tea."

"Why won't he have anything to do with her? What's wrong with her?"

"She's not a boy. Oz only ever wanted a son. Some men are like that. Even when Nick was alive, Olivia was just an optional extra."

"He's a bastard," Ross said with a violence that surprised her. "Where do you keep the teabags?"

Ross was the first to see Oz's car. The window of his bedroom overlooked the lane behind the house where they parked the Cortina. He clattered down the stairs and said that a grey car had just pulled in beside it.

No one ever parked there unless they were coming to the houses that backed on to the lane. It was nearly half-past twelve. Mrs. Kanaird gave Ross a plate of chicken sandwiches and pushed him out of the kitchen. He went back upstairs, making appalling jokes about family skeletons rattling in the attic and poor old Mrs. Rochester being a vegetarian. Heliogabalus, his eye on the plate, padded after him. The jokes upset Mrs. Kanaird. She was almost sure that Ross had a bottle in his room. His drinking was much worse that it had been.

Oz came through the gate from the lane. Mrs. Kanaird went to meet him. His eyes bulged behind the steel-rimmed glasses. He carried a briefcase under his arm and wore a cloth cap that clashed in colour and pattern with his striped shirt.

"Hello, Louisa," he said. "Are you going to fill in the pond? That's a pity."

"It's too dangerous with Olivia running around," Mrs. Kanaird said. "How are you?"

"All right." He didn't bother to ask how she was; she had the feeling that Oz valued the social graces at his disposal too highly to waste them on a woman who would shortly be his ex-mother-in-law. Nor did he mention Olivia. "Where's Lesley?"

"I'm here."

Lesley was standing in the back porch. Sunglasses masked her eyes and her mouth was set in a tight line.

Mrs. Kanaird tried to put the meeting on a more social footing. "Would either of you like a drink before lunch?"

"Not for me, thanks," Lesley said.

"A small whisky, please."

"Sorry—we haven't got any. Would wine do?"

Oz thought about it, then shook his head.

"I'll get on with lunch, then."

"We might as well get down to it," Oz said to Lesley. "No point in wasting time. Shall we go inside?"

"No—let's sit in the garden."

He frowned at her and then, evidently deciding that this point wasn't worth arguing about, followed her to the chairs underneath the plum tree. From the kitchen window, Mrs. Kanaird watched them talking. The window was open but they were too far away for her to hear what they were saying. Their faces gave nothing away. Mrs. Kanaird wished there was something she could do to help Lesley. She even prayed a little to a God whose existence she did not officially acknowledge.

While she watched and wished and prayed, she moved automatically about the kitchen. Her feet ached, and she wondered how many miles she had travelled over the years, from cupboard to table, from cooker to sink, from fridge to work surface. The daily drudgery of these repeated journeys had left its mark on the floor: the vinyl was pitted and worn; and in places you could see the stained concrete beneath. It all came down to money. Damn Oz.

Even the house in Muswell Hill was in his name alone, which suggested to Mrs. Kanaird that Oz had always thought of marriage as a potentially temporary commitment. Later, in her anxiety to leave Oz, Lesley had made too many concessions and signed too many pieces of paper.

Without telling Lesley, Mrs. Kanaird had consulted her own solicitor. She had asked him how one set about getting justice and how much it would cost. He stuck his thumbs in the pockets of his waistcoat and gave her a reassuring smile. And then he patiently explained that common sense, moral right and justice have very little to do with the legal processes that underpin the British way of divorce. All was well if both partners believed in these desirable qualities. But if even one of the spouses held other views, things could get very nasty indeed. It was quite simple, he said: the law was on the side of the wealthier and more ruthless partner. The best legal advice was never cheap; and moral scruples were quite frankly out of place in the divorce courts. In most cases, the solicitor concluded with a chuckle, the wife comes off the worse.

She looked out of the window again. Oz and Lesley sat close together but she fancied she could see the antagonism in their bodies, in the way their lips moved. Lesley had insisted on the meeting, but Mrs. Kanaird thought she was being over-optimistic. She would never be able to persuade Oz to pay any more than the bare legal minimum, if that.

"But it's worth trying, Mum," Lesley had said, smiling a little. "You never know till you try."

Suddenly Oz looked up at the house. He pointed and said something to Lesley. Mrs. Kanaird backed away from the window. Oz stood up and strode towards the back door, looking every inch like a man with a mission. Lesley followed. Mrs. Kanaird guessed by the set of her shoulders that the negotiations were not going well.

Oz barged through the kitchen and into the hall. A desperate need to reach the lavatory? He knew his way around the house—he and Lesley occasionally stayed here in the early days of their marriage. His feet thumped up the stairs. Oh God, she prayed, don't let him meet Ross.

Lesley came into the kitchen and took off her sunglasses.

"What on earth's going on?" Mrs. Kanaird said.

"It's Hell."

For a moment Mrs. Kanaird thought her daughter was describing her meeting with Oz.

"Heliogabalus," Lesley said irritably. "He's out on the drain-pipe. Oz has gone to rescue him."

Mrs. Kanaird understood at once. "That damned cat."

A drainpipe ran down from the guttering, passed within a few feet of Ross's window and made a seventy-degree turn that brought it just below the sill to join the main down-pipe on the other side of the window. For years the swallows had returned to the same nest in the angle where the pipe turned. At present it was occupied by the second brood of chicks. Heliogabalus had spent much of the summer staring up at the nest from the garden. Usually Ross's bed-room was empty, and the door and the window were closed. But not today. Mrs. Kanaird loved those swallows.

She followed Lesley up the stairs. There were thirty-nine steps, as in the book: three times thirteen, and therefore extraordinarily un-lucky; Mrs. Kanaird, like many agnostics, was well-versed in super-stitions and accorded them a wary respect.

"He got one of the chicks," Lesley said. "Didn't you hear the cheeping? The parents kept diving at him. And then he realized he couldn't get back."

"I hope he falls off," Mrs. Kanaird said. The lavatory flushed on the first landing. She jerked her head at the bathroom door. "You go on. I'd better warn Ross."

Lesley was almost at the top when the bathroom door opened.

"What's going on?" Ross said, swaying slightly. "Sounds like the bloody fire brigade on the hoof."

Mrs. Kanaird explained. Then: "Why don't you go in my room until he's downstairs again?"

"No way," Ross said.

He headed for the stairs. She realized that he'd reached the bel-ligerent stage. She hurried after him and put her hand on his sleeve.

"I'm not having Oz prying around my room." He had raised his voice; he was looking at her but not talking to her alone. "Besides I want to have a word with the little shit. Tell him a few home truths, eh? It's about time *someone* did."

At the top of the stairs, the door of the back bedroom was almost but not quite closed. Ross shouldered it open and stopped just inside the room. Mrs. Kanaird bumped into him and held on to his shoulder to steady herself.

Lesley was crouching by the window. Her arms were round her legs and her head was on her knees; it was as if she were trying to make herself as small as possible.

Someone screamed: it might have been a man or a woman: terror desexualizes its victims.

The window was a sash, and the lower half had been raised as far as it would go. Outside, against the grey, heavy sky, Mrs. Kanaird thought she saw a foot in a brown shoe. The foot was upside down and it vanished immediately. It was such an unlikely sight that her mind wanted to treat it as a hallucination.

The scream went on and on, changing in pitch and volume like a moving police siren.

A *thud* and a crisp *smack* filled the room. The sounds were joined yet perfectly distinct. There was a noise like tearing cloth.

The screaming stopped. The silence began.

Both she and Ross ran to the window. Lesley stayed exactly where she was. Mrs. Kanaird took firm hold of the sill and looked out. Ross pushed in beside her. Her eyes locked on to Heliogabalus: transformed into a streak of black fur, he shot up the gate as though it were a horizontal surface and disappeared through the gap between the top of the gate and the lintel.

"Oh Christ," Ross whispered. "Oh Christ."

THIRTEEN

"HELL CAME BACK at suppertime," Mrs. Kanaird said. "There was nothing wrong with him at all. He—he never misses his meals."

She sat silently for a moment. Her face was pinched as if with cold, and she rubbed her hands together on her lap.

"Tell us about Oz," Dougal said. The tiny voice-activated tape recorder in Hanbury's pocket was recording everything and silence was no use to them. "I realize this must be painful, but we need to know."

Do we need to know? he wondered. Will it ever help anyone?

"Oz?" Mrs. Kanaird picked a piece of fluff from her skirt. "He must have twisted as he fell. His head hit the corner of the paving stones, I think. The force of the blow must have . . ." She swallowed and looked imploringly at Dougal. "His body landed partly on the rubble and partly on Olivia's tricycle. Bent it out of shape: it's a metal one—we got it at a car-boot sale. It—I mean, Oz—he looked *broken*. I can't describe it."

"I presume you all rushed downstairs," Hanbury said, trying to hurry things along. "Was he killed outright?"

"Ross said so. He said that Oz couldn't have felt anything. But I'm not sure. In nightmares you always know when you're falling, you've got time to think about it, haven't you? Oz must have realized—"

"We shall never know." Hanbury's tone suggested that the uncertainty was something he could live with. "So what did you do?"

"Ross covered him with a blanket. I wanted to phone the police but Ross made me sit down." She looked defiantly at them. "My son was very kind, very thoughtful. We sat in the kitchen. Ross made tea, with lots of sugar. Lesley said it was an accident, that when she got to the room Oz was half out of the window, trying to reach Hell. And then he sort of lunged forward and overbalanced. Hell must have suddenly moved—or maybe he slipped on the pipe. There was nothing she could do. Can you imagine it? Someone like Oz losing his life for a *cat*. Does either of you have a cigarette?"

Hanbury pulled out a packet of Gitanes. She fumbled at it and the pack fell to the floor. Hanbury retrieved it and passed her a cigarette. He lit it for her, took one himself and, as an afterthought, offered the pack to Dougal.

"This is my first cigarette for twenty-three years," Mrs. Kanaird said, coughing. "Isn't it odd? The craving never really goes."

Dougal put an ashtray beside her. "You didn't go to the police in the end. Whose idea was that?"

"Ross said we had to think about this. He was the only one of us who kept a clear head. He said the police would automatically be suspicious because Lesley stood to gain so much, and because everyone knew that she and Oz had quarrelled."

"And what did Lesley say about that?"

"I don't think it had even occurred to her. She was terrified. The first thing she asked was whether they'd take Olivia away from her. And Ross said, of course they would if she went to jail. I can't tell you what it was like. The whole thing was a nightmare. I just couldn't think straight. Lesley kept saying they couldn't take Olivia away, that she'd kill herself first." Mrs. Kanaird looked from Dougal to Hanbury, her eyes pleading for them to understand. "I felt that we'd walked into a trap and there was no way out. What made it worse was that it wasn't our fault. If anyone was to blame, it was Oz and Hell. It's so unfair."

Dougal nodded, though in fact he disagreed with her. It was a common human failing to complain that life was unfair and then, with a magnificent disdain for logic, to blame someone else for this unfortunate state of affairs. He had never been able to understand why anyone should think that life was, or should be, fair; nothing in his own experience supported this idea. And there was rarely anything to be gained from blaming other people for what might be called a structural flaw in existence.

Hanbury was getting impatient. "You found a way out."

"It was Ross's idea. He suddenly came out with it: *you can't have a death without a body.*"

Dougal had worked out the essentials already but the details fascinated him. The story tumbled out in a torrent of words; Mrs. Kanaird needed to talk, and her frankness made him feel like a priest in a confessional.

Ross's idea was beautifully simple. Oz had come to have lunch in Halcombe on his way to Sheba's Tump. Very well, then, Ross said: Oz *would* go to Sheba's Tump and, having established his presence there, he would disappear. Apart from Lesley and Mrs. Kanaird, no one knew that Ross was in England. Wearing Oz's clothes and driving Oz's car he would go to the cottage, spend a few hours there, visit the pub to make sure he'd been noticed and then vanish. During the same evening he would drive up to Birmingham and dump Oz's car in a car park. By Sunday morning he should have been back in Dublin. By Monday he should have been in Istanbul.

"Oz would just vanish, you see," Mrs. Kanaird said. "They couldn't connect his disappearance with us. It'd be one of those unsolved mysteries like the *Mary Celeste*. I suppose they'd have frozen his estate—do you have to wait seven years until someone's presumed dead?—but Lesley and Olivia would have got it in the end, and I expect the courts would have given her some money to live on."

Dougal glanced at Hanbury, who was staring thoughtfully at the tip of his cigarette. Would the police have been so easily satisfied?

"Ross was wonderful," Mrs. Kanaird said. "So competent. He really surprised me."

There must have been something in it for him, Dougal thought:

possibly the promise of a future share in Oz's estate; more probably the proceeds from the sale of the diamond brooch.

Ross had moved the body into the pond, which had already been emptied. He had hosed away the blood and shovelled hardcore across the hole and the flowerbeds on either side. Luckily Oz had brought plenty of clothes and he had been much the same size as Ross.

"Ross was a little bit bigger," Mrs. Kanaird said. "The collar of the shirt was tight and the shoes pinched. It was just as well he didn't have to wear a tie. But Ross said he'd wear the cap and the yellow jacket when he went to the pub, and they looked all right on him. He said people would notice the jacket and the cap, not the face. And he was right, wasn't he?"

Hanbury looked surreptitiously at his watch. "It must have been quite a shock when Mr. Dougal turned up on Monday."

"Yes and no. It was sooner than we'd expected. And we thought it would be the police." Her lips quivered. She looked accusingly at Dougal. "You said the car was still there."

He nodded. That was how she had known that something had gone wrong, that Ross hadn't gone to Birmingham. "You drove to Sheba's Tump, didn't you? I suppose you'd been there before with Lesley and Olivia, so you knew the layout, knew where you could keep the car out of sight. But you couldn't find Ross. Then I turned up."

"And I ran away," Mrs. Kanaird said. "I just couldn't understand what he was up to."

The cigarette smouldered between her fingers. She had forgotten it, just as she had forgotten that Lesley and Olivia might return at any moment. When Lesley returned, the flow of confidences would dry up.

"Forgive me," Hanbury said, "but why did you and Lesley identify Ross's body as Finwood's? To an outsider it seems rather—ah—callous."

"We didn't have a choice. What would you have done?" She ground out the cigarette, twisting it viciously into the ashtray. "It was the worst thing I ever had to do. Have you got children?"

Hanbury said nothing.

Mrs. Kanaird sat back in her chair. "It seemed like fate, you know," she said in a brittle voice. "Nemesis or something. We'd tried to cover up an accident—and then Ross had a *real* accident." The implication—that Finwood's death might not have been a real accident—must have hit her as soon as the words were out of her mouth. She waved her hand, as though trying to brush the thought away. "What I mean is we'd been punished for trying to conceal Oz's accident. And part of the punishment was that I couldn't even admit Ross was dead. I couldn't say: 'Yes, this is my son.' I couldn't mourn him. I had to agree it was Oz. Because if I hadn't, the whole thing would have come out. We'd have been destroyed. All of us. Lesley would have gone to jail, and so would I as an accessory or whatever they call it. And what would have happened to Olivia?"

"I can see the dilemma," Hanbury said. "And—ah—please don't take offence if I mention this—there was a financial advantage in identifying Ross as Finwood."

"That never occurred to us," Mrs. Kanaird said angrily. "Look, my son was lying there *dead*. What happened to Finwood's money was the last thing on my mind."

"Of course, of course," Hanbury murmured. *"I* accept that, naturally."

"You mean the police won't?"

Hanbury shook his head, refusing to be drawn. "There's something you should know," he went on. "It is just possible—no more than that, I think—that your son's death wasn't an accident. And if that is so—"

A key turned in the lock of the front door. No one spoke. Olivia ran into the room.

Mrs. Kanaird muttered, "Not an accident? But that's impossible."

"Granny," Olivia shouted, "when we were at the rubbish dump, Mummy said she'd buy me a—"

She saw Dougal and Hanbury and ran back to the hall. Lesley came in, her eyes widening with surprise. Dougal glanced at Mrs. Kanaird: she was looking at her daughter.

"Hello," Lesley said with a cheerfulness that sounded entirely natural. "This looks like quite a party." She saw the ashtray by Mrs. Kanaird's chair. "Have you started smoking again?"

"They know, darling," Mrs. Kanaird said.

"Know what exactly?"

"About what happened on Saturday."

Olivia crept back into the room.

Lesley looked at her daughter. "It's time for lunch. You'd better wash your hands."

The phone rang as Edgar Timworth was forcing himself to eat a salad sandwich.

"Hello, Ed," Lesley said.

"Lesley, thank God. We've got to talk. That private detective came to see me. Dougal or something. He thinks Oz might have been *murdered*. Something about his boots not being muddy. I thought I'd better let you know."

There was a silence on the other end of the line.

"Lesley? Are you there?"

"You're too late," she said. "He and his friend have just left. Personally, I think they're making a mountain out of a molehill. But don't tell anyone else, will you? You know how gossip gets around."

"Of course I won't."

"I told them you were with me on the Saturday evening, and where we went. At least we're in the clear."

"Yes, yes," Timworth said impatiently. "Lesley, there's something else. Did Oz ever mention an author called McQuarm?"

Another silence. Then: "That's something we need to talk about. But not on the phone. Is there any chance you could come down this evening? You could spend the night if you want."

"That would be wonderful."

"When can you get here?"

"About six? I can leave work early."

"Perfect. If anyone asks why, you can always say it's to do with Oz's estate. And Ed—don't worry, will you? It'll be all right."

• • • •

Celia Prentisse was on the whole relieved when William phoned during the afternoon to alter their plans for the evening. Instead of her coming to his flat for dinner, he suggested that they went to a restaurant. He said he hadn't had time to cook. She disliked going to his flat at the best of times. It was like spending an evening inside his mind, which inevitably made her feel uncomfortable.

He collected her in the Sierra at seven-thirty. Usually he asked if he could look in on Eleanor, but he didn't tonight. On the way he said very little, apart from a string of questions about Eleanor, Valerie Blackstick and the job.

She made a complimentary remark about the car, which, she thought, would still have the status of a new toy for him; but he seemed uninterested in it. He drove carefully, she noticed, and rather better than he used to; perhaps practice was at last making perfect.

They went to Chalmer's, a restaurant in Twickenham where Celia had occasionally taken clients; the manager welcomed her and was quite put out when he discovered that she was not doing the entertaining. He gave them a table in a corner.

For the first time that evening she saw William in a good light. "What have you been doing with yourself?" she said. "You look almost as bad as you did—"

"After I found the body? Let's have a look at the menu."

Put out, she pretended to be absorbed by what Chalmer's had to offer. When she made a suggestion from the wine list, Dougal said she must have what she liked; he was drinking Perrier water.

"I'll have the same," she said. "What is this? A premature New Year's resolution?"

"I'm driving."

"That's never stopped you before."

"Celia—" He looked away.

"Sorry. What you do is your affair."

The waiter came to take their order. Celia chose the cheaper dishes on the menu, because William was paying; but apart from the prices she hardly noticed what she was ordering.

When they were alone again, William said: *"I'm* sorry. I should have cancelled tonight."

"What is it? Work? Would it help to talk?"

He shrugged. "If it wouldn't bore you."

"Don't be stupid. It's the same case? The boss's daughter and Finwood?"

He smiled at her. "I don't know why it's having this effect on me. I think in a way it's something to do with Eleanor."

Then he told her the outline of what had happened. She noticed with secret pleasure that he didn't place any restrictions on her; he took it for granted that she would impose them on herself and treat what he told her as confidential.

He made it sound very simple. Finwood fell out of a window. No one except Lesley would ever know for certain whether he had been pushed. Lesley's mother and brother helped her conceal the death. Ross posed as Finwood at Sheba's Tump. Ross died there; and it might have been an accident, apart from the fact that his boots weren't muddy as they should have been.

"What does Hanbury say about it?" Celia asked.

"He wants to let sleeping dogs lie. He only got into this because of Victoria Yarpole. At present she thinks that Finwood died at Sheba's Tump, and by accident. She made us continue investigating because two things worried her: this author, McQuarm, that Finwood was meant to have met on the day he died; and the fact that he didn't phone her on the Saturday evening."

"McQuarm?" Celia said. "Who's he?"

"God knows. James doesn't care. This afternoon he told Victoria that we'd traced McQuarm, and that he'd said Finwood had phoned to change the appointment to the following week. Oh, and he also concocted this story about the phone breaking down in the pub, to explain why Finwood didn't phone her as he'd said he would. Said he'd been to see the landlady. According to him, Victoria wiped away another tear and asked for a large brandy; she changed the subject and started talking about psychotherapy or something. As far as she's concerned, it's over."

"What would have happened if he'd told her the truth?"

"James thought she'd probably rush to the police. He had lots of quite powerful reasons for keeping her in the dark. For a start, it would make her even more unhappy than she is—though if you ask me, at least half her grief was playacting."

"You can't be sure of that," Celia said.

"If she'd really cared about Finwood, do you think she'd have accepted James's story?"

"Depends how good a liar he is. What were his other reasons for not telling her?"

"It'd ruin his career with Custodemus—he was quite frank about that. He also said that Finwood got what he deserved—and the man really *was* a nasty piece of work, by the way. He argued that the death of Ross was punishment enough for Mrs. Kanaird and Lesley. And then he tried to make me agree by bringing up Olivia: obviously, leaving things as they are would be better for her in every way."

"Well, I suppose he's right," Celia said. "About Olivia, I mean."

William glanced at her. "I didn't think *you'd* say that."

Celia felt herself flushing. "You thought I'd want justice at any price?"

"Don't you?"

Between them lay the memory of the time when Celia had chosen a sort of justice at the expense of her happiness and William's, and perhaps the unborn Eleanor's as well. William had committed a crime; and crimes should not go unpunished. The memory hovered between them, an invisible barrier like a sheet of glass. She imagined herself smashing through it with a clenched fist.

"Even if Lesley had pushed him," she said at last, "she wasn't doing it for herself. She was doing it for Olivia. And it was the same for Mrs. Kanaird: she *had* to help Lesley—what else could she do? I know they committed a crime, but it wasn't premeditated and it would be a worse crime to make them pay for it. And not just them —Olivia too."

"You've changed," William said. "You really have."

"It's something to do with having children, I think." She tried to laugh, to rob what she was saying of its seriousness. "It almost warps you—morally, I mean. And the worst thing is, I wouldn't have it any other way." She took a deep breath. "I'd steal for Eleanor, you know, if it were really necessary. Without a second thought."

"Yes," William said impatiently, as if she had stated something so obvious that it was hardly worth saying. "But would you kill for her?"

Celia shrugged. "Would you?"

"Probably."

She wanted to change the subject as quickly as possible. "Why would anyone want to kill Ross?"

William stared at her; she was afraid that he was going to insist on having an answer. *But would you kill for her?*

"Ross was a bit of a crook," he said. "Lived in Turkey. Mrs. Kanaird believes that no one knew he was back in England—no one except herself and Lesley. If she's right—"

"Ross was killed as Finwood?"

"Exactly."

"Nasty. And of course Mrs. Kanaird can't call in the police without landing herself and Lesley in trouble."

"She's an odd woman," William said. "Surprisingly tough. She realizes all that—but she still wants to know what happened to him. James was a fool to tell her." He ate in silence for a moment and then added: "She's got a diamond brooch. She's going to sell it."

"What are you saying?"

"She's hired us to investigate Ross's death. James is furious."

"Then why's he accepted the job?"

"Because he didn't have any choice. It's illegal to conceal evidence of a crime from the police. We're doing that already—we're accessories after the fact. She says if we don't help, she'll have to call in the police."

"But you said—"

"I know." William threw down his fork and reached for his rolling tobacco. "I think she's bluffing, that she'd never actually do it. But James isn't sure, and he's got too much to lose to want to gamble on it. He thinks she might not be entirely sane any more, so it's safer to humour her." William's fingers shook as he arranged tobacco along the cigarette paper. "Bizarre, isn't it? This morning we thought we had her over a barrel. But now, to all intents and purposes, Mrs. Kanaird is blackmailing us."

FOURTEEN

DOUGAL THOUGHT ABOUT HYPOTHESIS A as he drove slowly northwards up Gunnersbury Avenue.

Hypothesis A was beautifully tidy and trouble-free. It went like this: Ross had an accident on the way back from the Intemperate Frog. Or maybe he'd gone back to the cottage first and cleaned his —no, Finwood's—boots and then went out again for a breath of fresh air. He needed to wake himself up ready for the drive to Birmingham.

Dougal braked as a traffic light ahead turned red. At this time of the evening the roads were relatively clear and by now he knew this route between Kew and Kilburn as well as he knew anywhere in London. Perhaps he should have gone home another way, which would have forced him to concentrate on the practical details of driving and navigation. As it was, his mind was uncluttered; much as he would have liked to, he couldn't stop thinking about the case.

The only problem with Hypothesis A was the fact that Ross should have got as much fresh air as he needed on the way back from the pub. Also, why bother to clean the boots if he were planning to use them again immediately afterwards?

A picture of the Wellingtons at Sheba's Tump slid into his mind. They were green, with cream soles, and they'd looked new. A recent acquisition. People made jokes about green Wellies; they went with Volvo estates and large dogs and Barbour jackets; they were part of the pastoral disguise adopted by the urban middle-classes for weekend wear at their country cottages. Perhaps Victoria had forced Finwood to buy them: a significant stage in the greening of Oz.

Wellington boots made Dougal think of Olivia, which brought Lesley, an unwelcome and disturbingly frequent guest, into his mind; and she led by a connection whose nature he preferred not to examine to Celia. Celia had pecked at her dinner; she had dark smudges under her eyes and she hadn't wanted to talk about herself. She'd parried his questions about Valerie Blackstick, and he hadn't dared to raise the idea of his becoming a part-time nanny. The plan was a non-starter like Hypothesis B.

Hypothesis B was not only intrinsically implausible but also difficult to test. Ross, Dougal murmured to himself, has an enemy who follows him to Sheba's Tump and, perhaps on impulse, kills him. It was implausible because no one but his mother and sister knew he was there, and they had no reason to kill him—quite the reverse. It was difficult to test because they knew very little about Ross's past, about who might want him dead. Dougal tried and failed to imagine Julio or a vengeful Turkish tourist lurking in ambush at the top of the mound. This led to another point: Ross had decided to go there only a few hours before; and his killer would have needed either prior knowledge of the terrain or time to make a reconnaissance. Hypothesis B was a dead duck.

He signalled right and turned into Gunnersbury Lane. Hypothesis C was, at first sight, the strongest of the lot: the murderer intended to kill Finwood, not Ross, and still believed in all probability that he or she had succeeded.

It was no secret that Finwood meant to go to Sheba's Tump. Several people had obvious motives to kill him, among them Hanbury, Josephine Jones, Ed Timworth, Mrs. Kanaird and Lesley.

Under this hypothesis, Lesley and Mrs. Kanaird were automatically ruled out, because they alone knew that Ross, not Finwood, was at the cottage. Ed Timworth, however, might have killed Finwood, either to help Lesley or for another, more selfish reason. Timworth must know the geography of Sheba's Tump better than anyone. This afternoon, Lesley had claimed that she and Timworth had spent the Saturday evening together; the alibi was worth investigating. Like many weak people, Timworth had a streak of violence in him—deeply buried perhaps, but pressure could bring it to the surface. It was even possible that the police had misread the time of death—that Ross had died later than they thought, in which case Timworth's alibi for nine o'clock was irrelevant.

It was beyond reasonable doubt that Ross had died on that stack of scrap iron between the tump and the barn—otherwise the autopsy would have revealed that his wounds had been inflicted after death. Timworth must surely have known that beneath the protective screen of nettles the railings waited like rows of rusting teeth. But it did not necessarily follow that he was guilty of murder.

There might well be other candidates, for Finwood had not been a lovable man. Heading the list of unknown quantities was A. J. McQuarm, the man or woman whom Finwood was due to meet on the day he died.

Dougal realized with a shock that he had already got as far as Old Oak Lane. In front of him was Willesden Junction; on the right a massive car-breaking plant; and on the left the Freightliner Depot. Behind him was a solitary police car.

A, B, C, he thought, it's just a pretty pattern that means nothing. Probably we shall never know.

At this very moment Hanbury was almost certainly working out how to manufacture enough evidence to convince their new client that Ross's death was an accident. It wouldn't be easy because Mrs. Kanaird was less credulous and more intelligent than Victoria Yarpole.

The police car switched on its flashing lights. Dougal blinked at the rear-view mirror. The car overtook him and signalled him to stop. He pulled over to the kerb.

An officer walked slowly towards him. Dougal rolled down his window.

"Good evening, sir. You were driving rather slowly, weren't you?"

"Was I?" Dougal said vaguely.

The policeman bent down and peered into the car. The street-lights pitted his face with shadows. He looked ill.

"Yes, you bloody were," he said. "Let's see your licence."

Another officer got out of the car. He was carrying something. Dougal began to laugh. He was going to be breathalysed.

Next morning, Dougal took the tube into central London and paid an unannounced visit to Gasset and Lode.

It was just after nine o'clock. He was not at his best at this time of day but he knew he couldn't afford to leave it much later. The weekly Gasset and Lode editorial meeting took place on Thursday mornings.

Josephine Jones was in the office that had once belonged to Oz Finwood. Her body filled the chair behind the desk and seemed on the verge of overflowing on to the floor. She was going through the morning's mail with her secretary. Her eyebrows shot up when she saw Dougal.

"I want a word with you," she said. "Tried to phone you yesterday but you were out." She nodded at the secretary. "We'll finish those later. Shut the door behind you."

"You've been talking to Ed Timworth," Dougal said.

Josephine nodded. "And I think you owe me an explanation. By the way, I'm not sure we'll be needing you for *Suffer the Little Children*. Perhaps you'd send the typescript back."

Dougal gave her one of his professional cards. She glanced at it and tossed it in the waste-paper basket.

"Well?" she said.

"I was hired to look into Finwood's death," he said. "I couldn't tell you before because at first the client insisted on keeping the investigation secret. I didn't have a choice, I'm afraid. But I'm sorry."

"I do have a choice." Then her curiosity got the better of her. "But surely Oz died in an accident?"

"Probably he did. The police certainly think so. But the client's a bit overwrought. We're just checking out the loose ends. Like Mc-Quarm."

"And me?"

Dougal nodded.

"What happens if I turf you out?"

"Nothing very much. I can't make you answer questions. I don't think this will ever be a police matter."

Suddenly she laughed. "I can't get over it. You of all people."

Dougal was offended but he did his best to conceal it. "There might be a book in it one day."

"*Confessions of a Private Eye?* I suppose there might. Look, are you going to do *Suffer the Little Children?* Or was that just an excuse to get me talking?"

"Of course I will," Dougal said. "The Custodemus job is only part-time. The question is whether you want me to."

"I don't know who else would do it at such short notice. But you'll get it in on time? No last-minute delays?"

"Have I ever been late?" Dougal said.

"No. You're one of the few freelances who aren't. Why the hell am I a loose end?"

To his delight he realized that she wanted to be questioned. Some members of the public actually enjoyed it. This aspect of human nature, he had discovered, was one of the few advantages that lightened the lot of a private investigator. Answering questions, however mundane, not only made such people feel needed: it also brought a touch of romance, in the broadest sense, into their lives. The lure did not appeal to everyone and it was curiously difficult to predict whom it would attract. Intellectual sophistication or social class had nothing to do with it.

"As a purely academic exercise," he said, "we're trying to rule out anyone who might have had a reason to—"

"Murder him? Come off it. I loathed him—practically everyone did—but I wouldn't have killed him."

"You would say that," Dougal pointed out. "Wouldn't you? You got his job, which gives you a motive. You knew where he was going—"

"No. I knew he was going to Ed's place in Powys, but that's all."

She was warming to this for she went on: "I could have found out the address, of course. The only problem is, I didn't."

"Could you prove it? If you had to, I mean."

"Of course I could." She dug into her shoulder bag and produced a diary. "I was at a crime writers' conference in Newcastle that weekend. From Friday evening to Sunday afternoon."

Newcastle, Dougal thought, must be a good two hundred miles away from Middle Radnor, if not more. But how fast could you do the journey by motorway?

"Perhaps you slipped away on Saturday evening."

Her eyes gleamed. "In that case my double must have made the after-dinner speech. And I hate to think who got drunk afterwards. I didn't get to bed until three o'clock."

"Witnesses?"

She reeled off half a dozen names.

Dougal solemnly wrote them down. "All right," he said. "I'll tie a knot in you. What about McQuarm?"

"I can't help you there. The only person who can do that is Ed Timworth, and I don't think you're his favourite person at present. All I can tell you is that McQuarm's got another book on the stocks."

"You've had the outline?"

"Ed biked it round yesterday. *The Child of Russia.* Yukky title but we can change that. It's a sort of troika-and-vodka job in which the last of the Romanovs seduces the Soviet President. Except that the heroine's not really a Romanov at all but a Polish Jew from Texas. There's a subplot involving a conspiracy to blow up the White House but that's a fairly minor affair."

"Will it work, do you think?"

She grunted. "No reason why it shouldn't. It's going to be even more salacious than the last one."

"Tell me—you've read *Empire of Flesh and Blood:* on the basis of that, what would you say McQuarm was like?"

"That's an impossible question, and you know it. I remember wondering if he might work abroad, in business. Some of the detail seemed almost authentic—stuff like how you can avoid paying duty on imports or how you make currency transfers to Swiss banks. But probably it just means he did a little research on it, which made a nice change."

"He?" Dougal said desperately. "You think McQuarm is male?"

"I honestly don't know. Usually you can tell, especially in the sex bits. But not with McQuarm. It sort of goes both ways. You're looking for a hermaphrodite."

"Thanks," Dougal said. "That's a great help."

"Me?" Hanbury said. "Are you insane?" He stared not at Dougal but at a fat wasp which was trying to bore its way through the window to the outside world. "Whatever gave you that idea?"

"You told me to explore every avenue."

"I'm not an avenue," Hanbury said stiffly. "I'm your employer."

There was a knock on the door. His secretary brought in the mid-morning coffee.

"I've made the booking for tonight," she said. "Second row of the stalls."

"Good. Would you tell them to bring the car round in twenty minutes?"

When she had shut the door behind her, Dougal said: "It's a question of motive and opportunity. You want control of Custodemus, and Victoria can help you get it. But Finwood was in the way."

"You're grasping at straws."

Privately Hanbury was rather relieved: he had wondered whether something like this might be going through Dougal's mind, and he preferred to know precisely what it was.

"Convince me," Dougal suggested. "Just for the record."

"There won't be any record of this case. First, I had no idea that Victoria was seeing Finwood. She was keeping very quiet about him because of her father. So naturally I had no idea about this jaunt to Sheba's Tump. I—"

"She might have mentioned it to you without necessarily mentioning Finwood; and you might have been having her followed so you could have known about her affair with him."

"Well, she didn't and I wasn't. Anyway, it's a physical impossibility: I couldn't have killed him. At the relevant time I was with Victoria—at Winston Yarpole's birthday party."

"We can't be sure that we know the relevant time. The medical evidence wasn't that precise. It's just that the theory that the accident happened on the way back from the pub fitted in with the estimated time-frame."

"And do you really think," Hanbury said, "that after the party I changed out of my dinner jacket, drove down to Wales, dragged him outside and pushed him down a hill I didn't even know was there? It's nonsense. Besides, I don't believe he can have died much later than nine o'clock. Ross was going to Birmingham. Why should he hang about at the cottage?"

"Good point," Dougal said. "Of course you could have hired someone to kill him for you. If you had wanted him dead, that would have been much more likely. And it wouldn't have been something that would have presented you with any major problems."

That was unkind, Hanbury thought, and quite uncalled for. Dougal was referring to an earlier phase of his life, before Hanbury had inherited both money and a taste for respectability from a wife whose death he still, rather to his surprise, regretted. Things were very different now.

The memory of Mollie, his wife, caught him unawares. He could no longer remember her face, only the emptiness that her departure had left behind her. They had had so little time together. He stared out of the window and tried to distract himself by considering the wasp. Its movements were sluggish, as if it sensed that the summer had ended and death was near. By now it must have patrolled most of the surface of the glass. The stupid creature hadn't realized that the window was open at the top, that freedom was waiting for it a few inches away.

"I give you my word," Hanbury said at last, "that I didn't even know that Finwood existed. As for my arranging his murder, it's quite preposterous."

Dougal nodded with what Hanbury fancied was a trace of reluctance. "All right. I've tried to explore the avenue and as far as I can tell it's a cul-de-sac. How do you fancy Victoria?"

"I beg your pardon?"

"As a suspect, I mean. She knew where Finwood was—or rather she thought she did, which comes to the same thing if Ross was killed as Finwood."

"But why, for God's sake?"

"I don't know. Maybe Finwood had been unfaithful to her. She's probably spoilt enough to feel that she's got a perfect right to execute someone if they'd offended her. And if she *is* as unbalanced as that, she could have asked you to investigate partly to put her in the clear if something went wrong and partly because it amused her. Maybe she's got an appetite for cheap thrills, and bringing in a private investigator was like playing Russian roulette or something."

Startled, Hanbury considered the idea for a moment. "It's scarcely likely, is it? You've absolutely no evidence for it. The time-frame is against it—Winston's party didn't break up till after midnight. In any case, she would have realized it wasn't Finwood."

"But it was dark, remember? If they didn't talk, she might not have known. Besides, she might have hired someone to kill him, which would take care of the alibi as well."

"Assassination is not the sort of service you find in the Yellow Pages, William." Hanbury began to fold this morning's *Times*, which was lying unread in front of him. "She wouldn't have known where to begin. You're wasting time."

"Just exploring every avenue," Dougal said. "I think Josephine Jones is out of it. I saw her earlier this morning. I'll check the alibi, of course, but it looks rock solid."

"So." Hanbury steepled his fingers and prepared to recapitulate. There was a speck of dirt under one thumbnail, and it offended him. "We're back where we started. It looks like Ross Kanaird was killed because someone mistook him for Finwood. We have three possibilities." He ticked them off on his fingers: "A person or persons unknown, in which case we'll probably never know what happened. Edgar Timworth, the man with a guilty conscience about something, who unfortunately may have an alibi. And finally, of course, there's our old friend McQuarm." Hanbury stood up and, carrying *The Times,* moved slowly towards the window. "I'm not convinced that there's much point in our continuing with this. The real problem is how we deal with Mrs. Kanaird."

Dougal ignored this. "I did wonder," he said diffidently, "if in fact there were only two possibilities."

Hanbury frowned. He smashed *The Times* against the window. The wasp's broken body dropped to the floor, leaving a smear on the glass. "You mean that Timworth's alibi—?"

"No. I haven't checked that yet. But has it occurred to you that McQuarm and Timworth might be one and the same person?"

"I think I shall walk," Hanbury said, contriving to suggest that descending the stairs instead of taking the lift was a rather daring activity, like climbing down the north face of Everest. "My doctor advises exercise."

Dougal walked with him. He had noticed in the last year the steady advance of surplus flesh over Hanbury's body. Respectability was fattening. But how deep did the respectability go? Somewhere under the flab was the old Hanbury, sleek and ruthless. Once you had found it in you, was the capacity for murder something you could ever lose? Hanbury's defence boiled down to two points, neither of which impressed Dougal: that there was no positive evidence to connect him with Sheba's Tump and Ross's death; and that Hanbury claimed he had nothing to do with the murder.

"I'm going to Wimbledon," Hanbury murmured, tapping his briefcase. "This is my structure plan for the expansion programme. I estimate it will treble our turnover in less than four years."

Dougal grunted. He had heard it all before. Branches of Custodemus were to sprout in every civilized country across the globe. New specialist sections would grow like fungus on the parent body of the Private Investigations Division: Custodemus would have separate facilities for handling celebrity problems, hostage negotiations, the infiltration of religious sects, aircraft larceny and industrial espionage.

"The Americans have been specializing for years," Hanbury said. "It's the obvious way to go. Even Winston's beginning to see that the bottom's dropped out of matrimonial disputes. Divorce is far too easy these days."

"When will you be back?" Dougal asked.

"I'll be tied up for the rest of the day. You could phone me at home around seven. But don't make it much later than that. Victoria and I are going to the Barbican Centre."

They reached the ground floor. The security guard left his desk and stood by the door, ready to open it. Outside the car-park attendant was waiting with the Jaguar; it was a beautiful car, Dougal thought, as dark and sleek as its owner used to be.

"Whatever you do," Hanbury said, "don't get in touch with Mrs. Kanaird. I want to work out our policy first."

"I might have another word with Julio this afternoon. You never know, it might help."

"How?"

"Because there's just a chance he might have known that Ross was back in the country."

"A pretty slim one," Hanbury said. "But you're welcome to try. As long as you're tactful."

He swept out of the door, nodding his thanks to the guard. Dougal walked down the corridor to the small office he shared with a retired pathologist who came in only on Mondays and two part-time typists who usually did their typing somewhere else. To his relief the room was empty.

On his desk was an envelope stamped with the logo of the press-cutting agency that Custodemus used. After Tuesday's conversation with Josephine Jones, Dougal had put in a request for anything relating to *Empire of Flesh and Blood* and A. J. McQuarm over the last three months. Only six clippings had surfaced—two from the *Bookseller* and one each from the *Daily Mail,* the *Standard,* the *Sunday Times* and *Private Eye.* Only the last of these had anything new to tell him: *Private Eye* claimed to have heard a rumour that A. J. McQuarm was an unnamed politician who had been sacked in the last cabinet reshuffle.

Dougal picked up the phone and dialed Timworth's number.

"Hello?" It was a woman's voice.

"Is Ed in?" Dougal said, wondering if Timworth had acquired a secretary.

"He's not back yet. He's driving up from Gloucestershire. He phoned me earlier this morning and said he was just leaving. He shouldn't be much more than an hour. Can I take a message?"

The voice sounded artless and short of breath. A young woman, Dougal thought. She'd given him too much information and given it too easily; he hadn't even identified himself. Maybe not a secretary. Wasn't there a lodger, a cousin?

"Just say Jim rang from Gasset and Lode," Dougal said. There were two Jims in the editorial department, the copywriter and the non-fiction editor. "I'll try again this afternoon."

He broke the connection and punched in the number of Brassard-Prentisse Communications. The receptionist said Celia was busy. Dougal said so was he and that this was urgent. He gave his name and a moment later she was on the line.

"What's wrong?" she said.

"Nothing really. I wanted to see if you were okay."

"I'm fine. Look, William, I'll have to go. Someone sent out a press release with the wrong company's name on it. All hell is about to break loose."

"It'd be nice to see you," Dougal said. Immediately he wished the words unsaid.

"You saw me last night. Give me a ring this evening if you want."

"All right. I should be home by six. Give Eleanor my love."

She put the phone down on him. Dougal stared at the frosted glass of the window. Phoning Celia had been a mistake: he'd achieved nothing for himself and merely exasperated her. He hoped the office crisis would have died a natural death by six o'clock.

Someone sent out a press release with the wrong company's name on it . . .

The words reverberated in his mind. They meant something

more than they said, and he didn't know what. It was as if the sentence had set up an echo whose source he couldn't identify. His failure infuriated him.

The wrong company's name . . .

The words gave him another idea, which pushed the failure to the back of his mind. He grabbed his coat and almost ran out of the office. The security guard looked curiously at him as he plunged through the big glass doors into the street.

Luck favored him. As he reached the Strand, a taxi was just setting down a fare on the corner. Dougal scrambled inside. They drove westwards, cutting down to Victoria and then across Belgravia to Cromwell Road. Dougal paid off the taxi at Earl's Court and walked quickly through the streets to the mansion block where Edgar Timworth lived and worked.

This time the communal front door was closed and locked. Dougal pressed the bell for Flat 29.

The intercom crackled. "Hello?"

It was the same voice he'd heard on the phone.

"I've got an appointment with Ed," Dougal said. "Isn't he back from Halcombe yet?"

"Well, he's on his way but—"

"He's not back?" Dougal said with a pretense of amazement. "I suppose I'll have to wait for him. Can you let me in?"

She said nothing for a few seconds: time enough for Dougal to wonder if her common sense was telling her to be cautious.

"But who is it?" she said at last. "If you don't mind me asking."

"I'm one of his authors," Dougal said. "My name's McQuarm."

"McQuarm? Oh, I'm *so* sorry."

The intercom buzzed. Dougal put his hand on the door and it swung open.

FIFTEEN

ED TIMWORTH ran up the stairs, swinging his overnight bag like a skipping rope.

He felt sixteen again. He felt like a tightrope walker dancing joyfully on a high wire without a safety net beneath. Pale sunshine seeped along the second-floor hallway from the window at the far end. Love transfigured everything, even the stained beige carpet, worn along its centre by years of passing feet.

He let himself into the flat. Rachel was standing in the kitchen doorway. She put her finger to her lips and beckoned. Even at this distance he could read the excitement on her face. She wore her tightest jeans below a man's white shirt; the shirt was baggy on her, and its top buttons were undone to reveal her not inconsiderable cleavage. It was difficult to imagine anyone less like an invalid.

"I thought you had flu," he said. He had expected to find her hunched over a hot-water bottle in bed, with a thermometer and an array of patent medicines on the table beside her. Rachel was one of those people who throw themselves wholeheartedly into whatever situation they find themselves, including ill-health.

She drew him into the kitchen, which smelled strongly of recently-applied perfume and freshly-ground coffee.

"He's here," she hissed. "And I was in my *dressing-gown*. Why didn't you tell me he was coming? He's nothing like I imagined. I made him some coffee and put him in the office."

Timworth grinned down at her. Usually he found his cousin pro-
foundly irritating. Rachel had a selection of bad habits like talking
when he wanted to read and spending hours in the bathroom. She
was nineteen and young for her age; her emotional responses to life
were limited to joy and tragedy with nothing in between. This
morning, however, even her enthusiasm seemed attractive if only
because it was a pale and unfocused imitation of his own feelings.

"You can tell he's very intelligent," she said. "That's something I
like in a man."

In that case he could only assume, on the basis of the boyfriends
she brought to the flat, that she liked the absence of intelligence
even more. It was a matter of constant surprise to him that she was
intellectually capable of holding down her job as a filing clerk at the
Home Office. Her father paid generously for the rent of her room
and for the comforting if inaccurate knowledge that he, Timworth,
was standing *in loco parentis*. The financial contribution was no
longer necessary. He could afford to ask her to leave. In his present
mood he almost felt like letting her stay.

"You haven't told me who's here," he said. "And I could do
with some coffee myself."

"It's A. J. McQuarm, of course." Her eyes were round with
wonder. "He's really quite good-looking and not all that old."

"McQuarm?" he said in a voice that seemed unnaturally casual.
"He's here?"

"Well, you should know. You phoned him from Halcombe to ask
him round." She lowered her voice still further. "Actually, I think
he was a bit put out to find you hadn't turned up yet. He's been
here for nearly half an hour."

"Yes, of course," Timworth said wildly. "Halcombe. Yes, it took
me longer than I'd expected. There were roadworks on the M4."

"But why didn't you warn me?"

"I didn't know—I mean, I talked to him after I'd talked to you.
Anyway, I thought I'd get here first."

The lie spilled out of him before he had time to think. The glow
he had felt since leaving Lesley evaporated: in its place was a
clammy panic that stifled thought. Rachel was completely uninter-

ested in thirty-two of the thirty-three authors he represented. But she had been fascinated by A. J. McQuarm for nearly two months. One rainy Sunday afternoon when she was between boyfriends, she had picked up a proof copy of *Empire of Flesh and Blood*. She had sat on the sofa, for once ignoring the television, all afternoon and all evening. On the Monday morning she phoned work to say she was sick. She ploughed on until she finished. He had never seen her read a book before. Ever since then she had badgered him in vain for biographical details about the author.

"Coffee," Rachel said. "Here you are."

He looked blankly at her.

"You said you wanted some. Ed, are you okay?"

"I'm fine." He took the mug from her and wished desperately that he didn't have to handle this alone. At best, someone was playing a nasty little joke on him, making life imitate art. The worst didn't bear thinking about. "Well, I'll see you later."

"Ask him if he'd like some lunch. I could do an omelette or something. I'm quite good at those."

"We'll see."

He moved down the hall to the closed door of the office. Rachel twittered behind him, saying something about a choice of mushrooms or cheese fillings. The stupid cow had left the visitor alone in there for nearly thirty minutes. He glanced over his shoulder; his cousin was poised in the kitchen doorway, probably praying that McQuarm would demand another cup of coffee. He opened the office door.

In the visitor's chair in front of the desk sat William Dougal. He was reading one of the finished copies of *Empire of Flesh and Blood* which had arrived from Gasset and Lode on Monday.

"Hello," he said. "This is really rather good. The background detail's most impressive."

Timworth shut the door behind him. "What the hell do you think you're up to?"

Dougal shut the book, marking his place with the flap of the dust jacket, and laid it gently on the desk.

"I think that's my question," he said.

"Gaining entrance by false pretences is—"

"Ssh," Dougal said. "Unless you want your cousin to hear, I'd keep your voice down."

Timworth shut his mouth, opened it and shut it again. Unfortunately Dougal was right: Rachel was quite capable of eavesdropping. He walked round the desk, slopping coffee on the carpet. Anger writhed inside him, struggling to get out. But he couldn't afford to let it explode into violence any more than he could afford to phone the police. Either option would mean publicity for the McQuarm business. He hated Dougal.

"I had a little poke around while you were out," Dougal said. "A glance at the accounts. A look at your author files. You understand?"

"Hasn't that Yarpole woman had enough?" Timworth said. "What's she trying to gain?"

For an instant he thought he saw surprise on his visitor's face. But Dougal said, "You're getting a twenty percent commission from McQuarm, not the usual ten. That's unusual, isn't it? It suggests your services as an agent are unusual, too."

Timworth sipped his coffee. The mug left a wet ring on the desk. He swore and wiped it away with a paper handkerchief.

"In the accounts," Dougal went on, "the payments are made to "Author." At least I presume that "Author" means McQuarm because all your other authors are down by their own names. And then there's the correspondence file. It's rather slim, isn't it? But maybe McQuarm gets in touch by telephone. Or maybe you meet somewhere and hand over the cheques personally. Or perhaps you talk to him in the privacy of your own mind."

Suddenly Timworth gave a yelp of laughter. It erupted out of his throat before he knew it was there, as unstoppable as a bubble of gas in a bowl of water.

"You think I'm McQuarm? Dear God!"

"I think you made a deal with Finwood: you wrote the book, he took it on for Gasset and Lode and you planned to split the proceeds. A small-scale swindle. What was the original advance? Six and a half thousand? Cottage industry–level. But not exactly ethical, was it? Then the whole thing got out of control. Against all expectations, the book *was* a success. But neither of you wanted the truth to be known. I mean, a fraud's a fraud, even if it also benefits the victim, which in this case was Gasset and Lode. What happened then? Was Finwood trying to get a larger slice of the cake?"

Timworth rested his hands on the desk to stop them shaking. "You might as well know. Oz wrote the book. But I didn't even know that until Gasset and Lode had offered for it."

"You mean he sent it to you under the pseudonym?" Dougal said. "And the letter had an accommodation address?"

Timworth nodded vigorously. A second later he realized he had slid into a trap.

"Then it's odd that the letter isn't in the author file."

"I—I lost it. It was inadvertently thrown away."

"Like the copy of your reply," Dougal said dryly, "and the letter in which you relayed the Gasset and Lode offer to him. Come off it. You were in it from the start."

"All right," Timworth said. "I did know. Oz turned up one day with this typescript under his arm. At the time we both needed money. Oh, for God's sake, it started out as a joke."

"I'm sure Josephine Jones and Graham Grimes would find it very funny."

"But need this go any further?" Timworth heard the note of pleading in his voice and despised himself for it. "As you pointed out, no one's suffered by it. Anyway, Oz is dead and—"

"Yes," Dougal said harshly. "Finwood's dead. That's where I come in."

"But it was nothing to do with me. I spent that Saturday evening with Lesley. We were together from about seven until after midnight. You can ask her."

"What were you doing?"

"Just driving. She was restless, you see. She'd seen Oz and he hadn't been very helpful. In fact she was in quite a state. Just wanted to drive around and talk. Oh, we had something to eat in a pub outside Swindon. It's no use, I can't remember the name."

To Timworth's relief, Dougal didn't press him. Instead he went off on a tangent: "It can't have been easy for you when Oz and Lesley broke up. Somehow you stayed friends with both of them."

"Well, why not?"

Dougal shrugged. "When a couple separates, the friends tend to be divisible assets, like the house and the stereo system."

"It was never a problem. Oz knew I sometimes saw Lesley. I'd known her long before I met him. And of course Lesley accepted that Oz and I had a professional relationship as well as a personal one." Timworth hesitated. "I'm sorry, but is all this relevant? To your client, I mean."

"My client's interested in Finwood," Dougal said, "and in how he died. If you ask me, it was probably an accident. But you must admit there are loose ends. For example, where's the McQuarm file that Finwood took from Gasset and Lode? It's never turned up."

Timworth frowned. "Are you sure that Oz had it?"

"Not absolutely. I expect there's a perfectly reasonable explanation for that and for everything else. Perhaps we'll never know. What my client needs is reassurance, and that's what she's paying me to provide."

"Will you tell her about this?" Timworth's lips were dry but he didn't want to lick them; it was too obvious a sign of nervousness. "I mean, from your point of view, McQuarm's a red herring. Oz was McQuarm. He was going to visit himself. In fact he hoped to produce an outline for a sequel while he was on holiday. He was under a lot of pressure from Grimes."

"I'd agree," Dougal said, "but for one thing, and that's the fact you keep on lying to me. When did you realize that Oz wasn't McQuarm?"

"Look, I've just explained—"

"I talked to Josephine earlier this morning," Dougal said. "And just to make quite sure I checked your files. *The Child of Russia* must have come as quite a shock to you, I imagine."

"He—he must have posted the outline before—"

"Now, now," Dougal said. "Let's not get too speculative. I think we can safely assume that they don't have a postal service in heaven."

To his shame Timworth felt tears in his eyes. He blinked. His mind filled with memories of playground bullies and childhood humiliations. *You've got to stand up to them, old chap,* his father had said. *Just hit them back. A bully is always a coward at heart.* Even at the time Timworth had known that was untrue, that the bullies weren't necessarily cowards and that they actually wanted you to try to hit them back because then they could hit you even harder. Had his father knowingly lied, or was he merely stupid? The tears flowed over the lids and trickled down Timworth's cheeks. He reached for another tissue and blew his nose.

"Listen," Dougal said. "I need to know the truth. I'm not going to tell anyone unless it's relevant. But I have to know, and one way or another I shall."

"I need a solicitor," Timworth said. "I need—"

"If it's any consolation, I think you really believed that Finwood was McQuarm. And you went on believing it after he died. You only realized you were wrong when the outline and the accompanying letter turned up. Even then maybe you didn't guess who McQuarm is. But you know now, don't you?"

The bastard was goading him, Timworth thought, and gloating in his power. Past fused with present; this quiet, tidy room differed only in non-essentials from the corner of the playground beside the bicycle shed. Now, as then, he was beyond help and beyond hope. Only instinct was left.

His chair keeled over and thudded on the carpet. He was on his feet, shouting. The obscenities streamed out of his mouth in a high, cracked voice that belonged to someone else. He gripped the edge of the desk with both hands and lifted it.

Empire of Flesh and Blood slid down the smooth surface. Dougal seized it and jumped up. The desk toppled on to the floor with a crash that shook the whole building.

For an instant they stared at one another in silence. Dougal's body was poised for flight but his face was without expression. Timworth felt almost tranquil, as if his inability to control his actions had absolved him from all responsibility for them.

"Ed, what's wrong?" Rachel was shaking the door handle. "Are you all right?"

She opened the door. Dougal dived through the gap, pushing her against the jamb. Rachel's mouth gaped in a perfect O but no sound came out. Timworth collided with her in the doorway. Her body was soft and lumpy like a sack of cotton wool.

"Get out of my way," he said.

The front door of the flat slammed. Timworth's anger drained away, leaving a terrible desolation behind. The hardwood door shut out the sound of Dougal's running feet. Rachel clung to his arm; her breathing was shallow and rapid. He himself was gasping for air. In the sitting room the clock ticked in the centre of the mantelpiece, measuring time as it slipped away.

Come back, he wanted to say. *Please come back.*

Hanbury reversed the Jaguar into the driveway and parked with a precision that pleased him beside the Ferrari. A curtain twitched in the bow window on the ground floor.

Winston Yarpole's house was at the end of a cul-de-sac in the maze of roads between Wimbledon Common and the All England Lawn Tennis Club. From the outside it was nothing much to look at —just a semi-detached house, coated with pebbledash; it was indistinguishable from thousands of similar houses which speculative builders had put up between the wars. But appearances were misleading: as Yarpole's wealth increased, so had the house. It had grown upwards and sideways and into the garden at the back. Yarpole could have lived anywhere he wanted; but he preferred to stay here, near the tennis, in the house where Victoria had grown up and his wife had died. He lived alone with his housekeeper, who, according to Victoria, had once been his mistress.

Hanbury eased himself out of the car and frowned at the Ferrari. What on earth was Victoria doing here? She hardly ever came to see her father. The most obvious explanation was that Yarpole had changed his mind about women being incapable of understanding business matters and asked her to sit in on his meeting with Hanbury. That was not an appealing prospect. Hanbury preferred to

keep father and daughter in separate compartments; the one re-
quired different tactics from the other, and if you tried to mix the
tactics it was confusing for all concerned.

The front door opened. Victoria strode towards him. Her face
was very pale, all angles and wrinkles. For the first time, Hanbury
realized, he was seeing her without make-up, as she really was. She
wore a long, tightly-fitting grey coat that buttoned high at the neck,
and most of her hair was bundled out of sight in what looked like a
forage cap. She looked about as feminine as the beadle in the Burlington Arcade.

"I'm glad I caught you, James," she said. "I'm afraid I shan't be
coming tonight."

"But why not?" He knew he sounded aggrieved. Much thought
had gone into the programme for this evening. During the interval
he intended to make the first move that would promote him irre-
versibly from established friend to aspiring lover.

"Because I don't want to." She lifted her chin. "I'm going away
for a while."

"May I ask where?"

"You can ask," she said, "but I don't see why I should tell you."

"That's entirely up to you," Hanbury said. He was disconcerted
to find that his predominant emotion was one of relief.

"I've just seen my father," Victoria went on.

"I—ah—guessed that."

"I told him I want to play a more active role in the company. It's
time I started doing something with my life. It took Oz's death to
make me realize that."

"I'm sure he was delighted," Hanbury said.

"As a matter of fact he wasn't. But I've got voting shares so
there's nothing he can do to stop me. Nor can anyone else."

"Why should anyone want to?" Hanbury opened the driver's
door of the Ferrari. "Have a good trip."

Victoria climbed into the car and he shut the door. Without another word or even a glance she reversed down the drive, scraped
the wing on the gatepost and turned on to the road.

Hanbury watched her until she was out of sight. As the Ferrari rounded the corner at the end of the road, he shut his eyes. For an instant he saw the face of his dead wife as clearly as though she were standing beside him.

And Mollie was smiling. He remembered how she used to pat him as she had patted her dogs. "Good old boy," she used to say. "Good old boy."

"Is it worth it?" Lesley said, opening the fridge. "I mean, you can't bring him back."

"I know." Mrs. Kanaird slid the baking tray into the oven, closed the door and straightened up. "But think how you'd have felt if it had been Olivia. You couldn't just let it go. You'd want to know how she died. You'd want to know as much as possible."

"No, I wouldn't." With sudden violence, Lesley pushed a box of eggs into the fridge. "You forget. I've been through this."

"Oh darling, I'm sorry."

In her confusion Mrs. Kanaird hung the oven gloves on the hook reserved for tea towels. Lesley had never wanted to talk about Nick's death. She had been positively rude when the welfare officer from the Cot Death Research Appeal had tried to help.

"You've got to put it behind you," Lesley went on. "It's best for everyone. Especially now, when we've all got a chance of making a new start."

You may have a chance, Mrs. Kanaird thought, but I'm too old and too tired for new starts. Olivia, who was wheeling her new red bicycle up and down the garden, rang the bell on the handlebars and waved at her. Automatically, Mrs. Kanaird waved back.

"And think of the effect it has on me." Lesley's voice rose in pitch. The fridge door was still open; the shopping bag stood forgotten on the floor. "I don't want to be reminded of it. I just want to forget the whole thing. We need to get back to normal."

Mrs. Kanaird turned on the hot tap and squirted far too much washing-up liquid into the bowl. It would be easier to forget her own name than to forget Ross.

"You don't seem to have any problem in that direction yourself," she said. "Is that what you mean by normal?"

"What are you going on about?"

"You and Ed, of course. Are you going to get married?"

"Maybe. Is there anything wrong in that?"

"Seems a funny time to choose."

"For God's sake. Life has to go on. Anyway, Ed's been good to me and Olivia." Lesley's hand relaxed its grip on the top of the fridge. She shut the door and added in her normal voice, "Almost as good as you have."

"You don't marry people out of gratitude. Are you in love with him?"

"I haven't said I am going to marry him."

"He thinks you are."

She turned off the tap and began to clear the table. Lesley was methodically unpacking the shopping and putting it away.

"You could tell by the way he was acting at breakfast." Mrs. Kanaird said angrily. "The way he passed you the marmalade. And as soon as he got back to London he couldn't wait to phone you."

"There was a reason for that. He said that William Dougal's been to see him. This morning—apparently he was waiting when Ed got back."

Mrs. Kanaird frowned. "But why?"

"Because you're paying him to go round making a misery of other people's lives. That's why."

They stared at one another. The hostility in Lesley's eyes was almost more than Mrs. Kanaird could bear. She guessed it mirrored the hostility she herself was feeling. Families are like hothouses, she thought: emotions grow into unnatural sizes and shapes.

"Why didn't you tell me that before?" Mrs. Kanaird said gently.

"I'm telling you now. I wouldn't be surprised if Dougal turns up here this afternoon. Pursuing his enquiries to the bitter end. *Your* enquiries." Lesley touched her mother's arm—tentatively, as if fearing a rebuff. The hostility had faded from her face. "Look, Mum, can't you see? It won't help anyone, least of all you. They'll just take your money and make us all feel miserable. And it's morbid."

Mrs. Kanaird pulled out a chair and sat down. The kindness in

Lesley's voice and the touch of her hand brought her close to tears. She felt intensely vulnerable, at Lesley's mercy. It seemed a strange arrangement that parents should be emotionally dependent on their children, and equally strange that people so rarely mentioned it.

"Perhaps you're right," she said. "I hadn't thought it through properly. Trying to find out about Ross seemed somehow—I don't know—*separate* from us."

Lesley said abruptly, "It's not a matter of not grieving. But that's a private activity."

"I don't know what to do."

"Tell Hanbury and Dougal that you've changed your mind. It's your decision, not theirs."

"You're always so certain about things, aren't you?"

Lesley shrugged. "I wish—"

Outside, metal clattered on stone. Mrs. Kanaird held her breath for an instant that seemed to exist outside time, waiting for the inevitable result. It was almost a relief when, at last, Olivia screamed in pain and perhaps outrage.

And then the front-doorbell rang.

"Tell him to go away," Lesley said as she ran outside.

Mrs. Kanaird walked slowly down the hall, giving herself time to rehearse the words she wanted to say. It was a pity that you couldn't treat a private investigator as you would a passing Jehovah's Witness or a door-to-door salesman.

"Not today, thank you," she said aloud.

She braced herself and opened the door. But it wasn't William Dougal or James Hanbury. A tall, grey figure was standing on the doorstep. At first Mrs. Kanaird thought it was a strange man.

"I've come to see Lesley," Victoria Yarpole said. "Will you let me in?"

SIXTEEN

"MY PSYCHOTHERAPIST called it a watershed experience," Victoria Yarpole said. "The death of a loved one so often is, don't you think? The living have to come to terms with it, to redefine themselves. Death is the ultimate index of life's value. Above all, he said, it is a time for psychic stocktaking. And it's absolutely fatal to deny the primacy of one's emotions."

"I'm sorry," Lesley said, "but I still don't understand what you want."

Victoria threw herself into a chair. "A rite of passage, I suppose. For all of us—you, me, Oz. That's the trouble with our society. We've taken the ritual from the great milestones of life. We must put it back, for our own sakes."

"Oz's funeral was on Monday. That was a ritual, surely?"

"An empty one. A pale shadow of what it should have been. A funeral should be a time for mourning, a time for forgiveness. And also a time for rejoicing, of course: Oz brought so much happiness into the world."

Lesley stared at her red lace-up boots and wondered if she and Victoria were talking about the same person.

"I've been very wrong, I can see that now." Victoria patted her breast, still tightly restrained by the grey coat, in what was presumably a ritual expression of guilt. "At first I converted my grief for Oz into hostility towards you. That was very, very immature of me.

I clung to my negative emotions about you when I should have embraced the healing process of grief."

"You mustn't let it worry you," Lesley said. "Naturally you were upset. But it's all—"

"I only came to my senses when I realized how groundless my suspicions were. And how deeply insulting to you. I've come to apologize."

"There's nothing to—"

"And also to ask a favour. Or perhaps to make a suggestion. We can help one another. At different times we both loved Oz. I know you had your differences with him. But death should be a time of reconciliation for both the dead and the living."

The doorbell rang.

"Just talking about him together would be a form of farewell. A sort of leavetaking."

Lesley heard a muffled squeal from Olivia in the kitchen. Mrs. Kanaird's footsteps passed the sitting-room door. The murmur of conversation outside was drowned by Victoria's loud and breathy voice.

"If we take it in turns to share our memories of him, to talk about how he has affected our lives—"

Two sets of footsteps were coming back up the hall towards the kitchen. "But I think we should talk about it first," Lesley heard Dougal say. Talk about what? Closing the investigation?

"—and to redefine the past we shared with him in the light of his tragic death."

"It sounds rather morbid."

"Not at all. Don't you see? Oz's death has already changed how I think of my life. I want to do something positive with it. The past is so terribly important for the sake of our *futures.*"

"I'm sorry, I don't agree." Lesley stood up. "The more you live in the past, the less you live in the present. Now if there's nothing else you—"

"No, *please.*"

With a moan, Victoria scooped herself out of the chair and stood up. Lesley recoiled.

"Just give me a little time. You owe it to yourself, you know. You need it. I can see the tension in every muscle."

Suddenly it occurred to Lesley that she was faced with a choice between two evils. Either she had to accept the temporary discomfort of a tête-à-tête with Victoria or she had to run the risk of Victoria meeting Dougal. And even Victoria could be trusted to draw the obvious conclusion from such a meeting: that Custodemus still had an interest in a case that was meant to be closed. Lesley looked up at Victoria and forced a smile on her face. Dougal would soon be gone for ever, which in one way was a pity. In the meantime it was essential to keep Victoria occupied.

Lesley nodded gravely, miming graceful submission to the force of superior argument. "I must admit you're right about the tension," she said. "And I haven't been sleeping properly either."

"Nor have I." Victoria sighed. "Sometimes one feels so dreadfully lonely. Do you?"

"Yes," Lesley said. "I do."

"So you see," Mrs. Kanaird said, "there's really no point in continuing."

"But don't you think you might regret it?" Dougal said. "Are you really sure you want to?"

Mrs. Kanaird smiled brightly at him. She had expected him to be relieved to drop the case, and his reaction worried her.

"Quite sure, thank you. You must send me your bill, of course."

Olivia pawed at Dougal's knee. "Come and see my bicycle."

"Why not go and play outside?" Mrs. Kanaird suggested to her.

"Don't want to. Can I have another biscuit?"

"No."

Mrs. Kanaird now regretted offering him tea; it was the natural thing to do when a visitor turned up in the afternoon, but Dougal had outstayed his welcome. It was almost as if he were making his cup of tea last as long as possible—as if he were hoping to see Lesley before he went?

The presence of Olivia was making things worse. Much of the conversation had to be conducted in hints and euphemisms. You could never predict what Olivia would remember or how much she would understand. A third problem was the visitor in the sitting room. It might cause difficulties for all of them if Victoria Yarpole realized that Dougal was here.

"Why's Victoria Yarpole here?" Dougal asked.

Mrs. Kanaird's cup rattled against the saucer. "How did you know it was her?"

"I recognized the car."

She had parked in St. Stephen's Street, directly outside the front door on a double-yellow line.

"I think she's here to bury the hatchet, as it were." Mrs. Kanaird glanced at Olivia, who was trying without subtlety to purloin a biscuit from the plate, and hoped that her granddaughter's vocabulary did not yet include the phrase. "It might be—er—unwise for you to meet her."

"Why?" Olivia said. "Who's Victoria?"

"Put that biscuit back," Mrs. Kanaird said.

"I can see that." Dougal sipped his tea. "But—"

The doorbell rang once more.

"Oh *God,*" Mrs. Kanaird muttered. She stood up. "I won't be a moment."

Olivia seized her opportunity. "You can see my bicycle now."

"Olivia, I'm sure Mr. Dougal doesn't want to—"

"That's all right," Dougal said. "I'd love to."

Olivia opened the door and ran through the porch to the garden. Dougal followed. Clara and Heliogabalus slid into the kitchen. Mrs. Kanaird shrugged and walked down the hall. Suddenly everyone else's concerns—Olivia's and Dougal's, Lesley's and Victoria Yarpole's—seemed remote from hers. She was very tired.

Mrs. Portnum was waiting on the doorstep. She had already unbuttoned her coat.

"Hello, Louisa," she said, edging herself on to the threshold. "I was just passing and I thought I'd pop in and have a word about the Church Appeal."

• • • •

From the west, billowing clouds the colour of charcoal were advancing across the sky. The grass was strewn with dead and dying leaves from the apple trees next door.

"Look," Olivia said. "It's mine. It's a boy's bike."

The red bicycle stood on the glistening flagstones above Oswald Finwood's grave. Olivia pointed out the two smaller wheels on either side of the rear wheel.

"In case I fall off," she said. "Do you fall off?"

"Sometimes," Dougal said.

The bicycle had reflectors at the front, at the back and on the pedals. The bell made a very loud noise. There was a basket at the front and a saddlebag at the back. All these things had to be admired.

"Push me," Olivia ordered.

Dougal lifted her on to the saddle and trundled her down the path to the bottom of the garden and back. The technique of steering was something she had not entirely mastered. Twice she fell off; but fortunately he was able to catch her the first time, and the second time she made a soft landing on a freshly-dug flowerbed. Olivia might be an intellectual prodigy but physical co-ordination still presented her with a few problems.

"Again," Olivia said when they reached the house.

"I'm tired." As he rubbed his aching back, Dougal noticed that she was wearing her indoor slippers, which now had a good deal of outdoor mud on them. "Shouldn't you be wearing shoes or boots or something?"

"No. If you push me, my slippers won't get dirty."

"They're already dirty," Dougal pointed out.

She gave him a look that meant *In that case why bother changing them?* and said, "Go on."

Instead, Dougal lifted her off the bicycle and into the back porch. He suspected that force was the only adequate answer to Olivia's brand of logic. Three pairs of Wellington boots stood on an old copy of the *Sunday Times*'s main news section; the newsagent had written the name "Kanaird" at the top of the newspaper, which answered one small question in Dougal's mind. The black boots with discoloured white toecaps probably belonged to Mrs. Kanaird; Lesley's must be the rather dashing dark blue pair with cream piping; and between them, looking dwarfish, were the tiny red boots decorated with tigers.

For a moment he thought Olivia was going to protest. But she sat down on the damp flagstones and extended her legs. "Now you'll have to give me another ride," she said.

He took off her slippers and put on her boots. "You're a realist, you know," he said. "You keep your eye on the main chance." He sniffed. "Can you smell something?"

"Push me," she said.

"Just a moment."

Dougal was desperately looking around for something to wipe the slippers on. It was becoming increasingly clear to him that one of the slippers wasn't merely muddy: no doubt Clara and Heliogabalus rated freshly-turned earth as superior natural cat litter. In the house, a door banged. One of the visitors must have gone.

"*Push me,*" Olivia ordered.

He left the slippers on the newspaper. It was simpler to obey her.

"Tomorrow," Olivia said in a gentler voice, "Mummy's going to paint my name on my bicycle. I want to have my name on all my things."

"Why?" Dougal said.

"To show they're *mine.*"

In one abrupt movement, Dougal let go of the bicycle and straightened up. A few words of Celia's leapt through his mind with the speed of an electric spark. Olivia, turning to look at him, twisted the handlebars. The bicycle swung sharply left. The front wheel dropped into a flowerbed and she toppled headfirst into a rosebush.

And in the silence before Olivia started to cry, he realized that Mrs. Kanaird was standing in the porch. To his surprise she was looking at him rather than at her granddaughter.

"Would you mind slipping into the lane for a moment?" she said in a rapid undertone. "Victoria Yarpole wants to see the garden."

Then the howls began.

• • • •

"I feel we've made a wonderful start," Victoria said, holding out her hand. "And you will come to London soon, won't you?"

Lesley took the hand. Victoria groaned with sisterly affection and swept her into a bony embrace.

"There's so much we haven't talked about. I think Oz would have been so pleased, don't you?"

Lesley gently disentangled herself. "Drive carefully."

Victoria removed the parking ticket from the windscreen and clambered into the Ferrari. Lesley shut the front door. She walked slowly down the hall to the kitchen, where her mother was giving Olivia her tea.

"Like a French farce, was it?" Mrs. Kanaird said. "Mrs. Portnum on the doorstep, that woman in the sitting room and Dougal in the garden. Two down, one to go. If you ask me, Victoria Yarpole's just plain nosy."

"Nosy-posy, nosy-posy." Olivia banged her spoon on the table. "Her nose is bigger than an elephant's."

"That's enough," Lesley said mechanically. "Where are your slippers?"

"In the porch. Mummy, they've got cats' poo on them."

"And how did that happen?"

"I don't know."

Olivia shovelled a spoonful of baked beans in her mouth in an attempt to close the subject before it reached the awkward stage. For once Lesley let her get away with it. If anyone had got rid of Victoria it was Olivia, whose imperious demands first for comfort and then for food had effortlessly overridden both the healing processes of psychotherapy and the discussion of Oswald Finwood's many virtues.

"Dougal's still out there," Mrs. Kanaird said. "Would you let him in?"

Lesley opened the back door. He was waiting in the porch. His hair and shoulder were sprinkled with rain.

He smiled at her. "Has she gone?"

"Yes, at last. I'm sorry about that."

"I've told Mr. Dougal that I've decided not to continue with the case," Mrs. Kanaird said. "He quite understands."

Dougal glanced from Lesley to her mother. "You're absolutely sure?"

They spoke at the same time. "Yes." "Quite sure."

"Then do you mind if I use your phone?" Dougal said. "I should let my boss know."

"Of course. You know where it is—in the sitting room."

He slipped away. Mrs. Kanaird began to butter a piece of toast for Olivia. Watching her made Lesley feel redundant. This was a familiar sensation, as irrational as it was powerful. She felt that her mother had somehow usurped her own position, that Mrs. Kanaird and Olivia could manage together perfectly well without an intervening generation between them. They didn't need her. Lesley muttered something about getting a jersey and left the room.

The sitting-room door was closed. On the other side of it, Dougal said loudly, "Can you hear me?"

Lesley paused at the foot of the stairs.

"Yes—it's an awful line . . . Is that the Intemperate Frog? . . . May I speak to Mrs. Angram, please?"

In the public relations industry everything moves at such speed, and everyone has such a short span of attention, that even crises tend to be short-lived affairs.

Celia had spent the morning and most of the afternoon on the phone, alternately soothing the managing director whose company's name hadn't appeared on the press release, and dictating the revised version to the magazines most likely to use it. It galled her to have to apologize continually for someone else's blunder. The real culprit was a junior account executive whose inability to recognize the existence of deadlines had already cost him his job.

At least she had been able to limit the damage. She had called in favours and made reckless promises to predatory editors. Until the magazines actually appeared, she wouldn't know for certain how successful her efforts had been. In one case she had failed, because the magazine in question had already gone to press.

At four-thirty, Hugo Brassard, her partner, shambled into the office and draped himself in the usual spiderlike pose on the corner of her desk.

"Well done," he said. "You look shattered."

Judy appeared in the doorway with a folder of letters for Celia's signature. "Like you've had a hard night on the tiles," she agreed. "You need to catch up on your beauty sleep."

"Eleanor's teething," Celia said weakly, holding out her hand for the folder. "I was too late to stop *Admiral 64 Plus* from using it."

"It doesn't matter," Hugo said. "No one who owns a piddling little home computer like the Admiral 64 will even know what a thirty-megabyte hard disc is. They certainly won't care who makes them. Why don't you go home?"

"Good idea," Judy said.

"Stop mothering me." Celia leafed through the folder, signing each letter. "I've got to rough out a release for George Venn. And then there's the artwork for—"

"Leave it," Hugo said. "There's nothing that can't wait. Go home and get a good night's sleep."

With Eleanor on the premises? Brassard was a bachelor who had no idea what a baby did to your routine. Celia closed the folder and gave it back to Judy. Her eyes itched with tiredness. She wanted to take out her contact lenses and lie in a warm bath. Then she wanted someone else to cook her a meal and to put Eleanor to bed and to wake up in the night when Eleanor decided that she needed company.

"All right," she said. "I'll go home. Why not?"

Hugo and Judy shooed her out of the office and down to the car park. Their solicitude touched her. I don't deserve it, she thought. She drove slowly home to Kew. The traffic was heavy but it lacked the rush-hour intensity she usually faced. She backed the car into the drive and tried to remember when she had last got home from work before five o'clock.

The sitting-room light was on. As soon as Celia got out of the car she heard the music. She unlocked the front door. "Oh Carol," someone was singing, "don't ever give your heart away."

The music was coming from the sitting room. This irked her because she had always thought it understood that the sitting room was her private territory. Celia poked her head inside. No one was there. She walked down the hall to the kitchen.

Eleanor was lying on the floor and eating a dishcloth. She was still wearing the Babygro she had worn last night. Valerie Blackstick stood with her back to the door, stirring a saucepan on the stove. Suddenly Valerie glanced down and saw what Eleanor was doing.

"Stop that, you little bastard," she yelled.

With one hand she snatched the dishcloth away. With the other she slapped Eleanor's leg with such force that Eleanor spun round on the vinyl-covered floor. Still crouching, Valerie looked up at the door and saw Celia. In other circumstances the dismay on her face would have been comical.

Celia seized Eleanor, who was crying furiously, and cuddled her. She backed out of the kitchen and into the sitting room. "Oh Carol" was still thumping out of the speakers. Crooning meaninglessly, Celia rocked her daughter to and fro in time with the music. Eleanor's nappy needed changing.

Valerie Blackstick tapped on the door.

"Look, I'm sorry," she said. "I can explain this. For a start I'm suffering from premenstrual tension, and my—"

"Get out," Celia said, softly because she didn't want to disturb Eleanor by shouting. "Out of this house, out of this job. *Now.*"

"You don't understand." Valerie Blackstick took a step into the room. "That was a one-off. I'm under a lot of strain."

"The only thing to understand," Celia said, "is that I want you to pack your things and go."

"If you insist." Valerie strode across the room and ejected the tape. "This is mine," she said in an argumentative tone, as if expecting or even hoping for disagreement.

"How soon will you be gone?" Celia said.

"Tomorrow morning okay? I'll need—"

"No, it's not. I want you out this evening."

"But what about my salary?"

"I'll discuss that with the agency," Celia said. "And, believe me, that'll be a pleasure. Now, when can you leave?"

Valerie sneered at her. "I'll be glad to get out of here. Two or three hours? Is that soon enough for you? I'll have to wait until my boyfriend can collect me."

Your boyfriend, Mrs. Danvers?

Without another word Valerie left the room and clumped into the kitchen. Celia heard the ping of the telephone extension and, later, Valerie going up the stairs and moving around overhead. Eleanor stopped crying and smiled. Celia smiled back through her own tears. She knew that she was tired and overwrought; she also knew that Valerie made her feel like a prisoner and that she didn't want to stay in the same house as her, even for a few hours. Nor did she want to be alone.

"Dada," Eleanor said. "Dada."

This was no time for nursing damaged pride. Celia picked up the phone and dialled William's number. There was no answer, of course, and she hadn't really expected one; he had said that he wouldn't be home until six o'clock.

Damn you, she thought, damn you for being right about the Blackstick, and damn you for not being there when I need you. She bit her lip to hold back the tears.

Valerie's tape recorder came to life. The opening bars of "Route 66" thumped and thudded through the house more loudly than ever before. Then the singer—Mick Jagger, she supposed—suggested that she should go his way if she ever planned to motor west.

Not west—but why not north? Celia looked at the clock on the video. It would take her well over an hour to drive across London to Kilburn at this time of day. Stupid, really. And William might be late. On the other hand she knew his neighbour in the flat above, and knew that William had given him a spare key.

"What do *you* think?" Celia said to Eleanor. "Crazy, isn't it? Here we are in the comfort of our own home. And I think we should go out in the rush hour and look for your father."

"Dada," Eleanor said. "Dada."

SEVENTEEN

LESLEY OPENED THE FRONT DOOR and said quietly, "You're going to get very wet. Have you got far to go? Where's your car?"

By now the rain was pouring out of the sky. On the other side of the road multi-coloured fragments of light glinted through the grimy stained-glass windows of St. Stephen's Church. Dougal shivered and turned up the collar of his jacket.

"In the car park behind the supermarket," he said.

"Here, take this." She held out a collapsible umbrella. "You can keep it if you want."

"Thank you. Or I could drop it in on my way home."

"No, keep it," she said irritably. "It's an old one. I never use it."

Their hands touched as Dougal took the umbrella. He shook it open. Jaunty yellow flowers flared against a turquoise background, and one of the spokes was bent.

They said goodbye. Hunching his shoulders, Dougal walked away. He wondered what they were saying about him in the kitchen. How much would Lesley explain to her mother? Maybe she never explained anything to her. The real question, perhaps, was how much had Mrs. Kanaird guessed. And how much was she pretending not to know?

The wind tried to tug the umbrella out of his hands and drove gusts of rain underneath it. In the Market Place the narrow pavements were crowded with last-minute shoppers and people rushing home from work. The rain gave everyone an air of desperation.

Beside the supermarket an alley led down to the car park. A man in a brown coat was shunting the wire trolleys together; the rain had stained his coat black and he swore as he worked, cursing monotonously and impartially the trolleys that were too misshapen to slot together and the pedestrians that got in his way.

The car park was full of revving engines. The weather had made it so dark that most of the moving cars had their headlights on. The interior of the Sierra was dry and out of the wind. Dougal took off his jacket and switched on the light above the windscreen. He wiped the worst of the rain from his face and hair with paper handkerchiefs. What he really wanted was strong black coffee. Instead he rolled a cigarette.

Before he had time to light it, there was a knock on the nearside window. Dougal dropped the cigarette. On the other side of the rain-streaked glass hung a severed head levitating a yard above the ground. The blurred features were Lesley's.

A fraction of a second later, he realized that the rest of her body was either concealed by the car door or camouflaged by the gloom. Instinctively he groped for the car keys, which were already in the ignition.

She rapped on the window again. Dougal changed his mind, leant across and opened the passenger door. Lesley climbed into the car.

"Thanks," she said casually. "It really is filthy out there."

She was wearing the blue Wellington boots and a dark green plastic raincoat that billowed round her like a cloak. She was panting slightly, probably because she had been running. The coat somehow diminished her into the small, pretty child she had once been. She pushed the hood off her face and looked at him.

Dougal bent down to pick up the cigarette. "And what can I do for you?"

"I wanted to talk to you. It was impossible at home."

"What did you tell your mother?"

"About what?"

"About coming out now."

"I said I needed a breath of air. I said I felt trapped in that house and I wanted to scream and would she mind looking after Olivia." Lesley hesitated, but it was as if the words wanted to come out; they wouldn't let her stop. "And she said yes, because she's always been an unselfish person, and she's used to me being selfish. It's all relative, this selfishness. I mean, Olivia is always going to be selfish with me, and I'm not with her. I'm sorry—I didn't mean to bore you with all that."

Dougal rolled down the window an inch and lit the cigarette. So she hadn't wanted her mother to know. Of course not. Depression hovered over him. He stared at the windscreen because he didn't want to look at Lesley's face.

"What do you really want?" he said.

"Will you drive me to London? I hate this place."

Dougal asked a question, any question, to give him time to think. "But what about Olivia and your mother?"

"I'll phone them on the way—say I've gone to see a friend. My mother will love it. She grumbles like hell about having Olivia around, but she adores it really. Especially when I'm not there to cramp her style. It's like she's been given a second chance."

"All right. Where do you want to go exactly?"

"I'll go and see Ed, I suppose."

"Are you in love with him?"

"What's it got to do with you? No, I'm not. Can't we get moving?"

He put on his seatbelt and started the engine. Neither of them said anything else until they were out of Halcombe.

Lesley stirred in her seat; the plastic raincoat rustled. "I'd thought you'd want to ask me lots of questions. Or aren't you interested any more?"

Interested in the case or interested in her? An unexpected spurt of anger dispelled the depression.

"I don't think you can tell me much," he said. "You wrote *Empire of Flesh and Blood,* didn't you?"

"What makes you think that?" She sounded genuinely surprised, which meant nothing because he already knew that she was a good actress.

"Timworth thought Finwood wrote it. I think he believed that until very recently. This morning he tried to convince me that he still does think that." He changed down and accelerated past a small lorry. "You should have waited before you sent him the outline for the second one—waited till the fuss had died down. He tried very hard to protect you. I don't think he'd have done as much for anyone else."

"Oh, come on," Lesley said. "That doesn't prove I wrote it."

"Why did he come and see you yesterday?"

"That was about Oz's will. As you know, he's the executor. Anyone could have written that book, and you know it. Even Oz could have done it. Maybe someone else wrote this new outline."

"I imagine you used the carrot-and-stick technique on Timworth. Not in so many words, you wouldn't be so unsubtle. The carrot was romance and of course a continuing share of the profits. The stick was your threatening to expose the original fraud that he and Oz set up."

"You're not making sense," Lesley said. "There's no evidence that Oz didn't write *Empire of Flesh and Blood.* Can't you get that into your head?"

"The McQuarm author file from Gasset and Lode still hasn't turned up. Odd, don't you think?"

"What's that got to do with it?"

"Oz had it when he died. No one admits to having seen it." He glanced at her profile. "Anyway, why did Oz come and see you on the day he died?"

"To talk about Olivia. You know that."

"Up till then you'd been talking through your solicitors. No, there was something else. Do you ever see the *Sunday Times?*"

"Occasionally. I prefer the *Observer.*"

"Your mother doesn't. She's got it on order from her newsagent. The Sunday before Oz died there was a gossip item in the books section. A snide little piece about Gasset and Lode maintaining their reputation for schlock, and about how no one was surprised that the author of *Empire of Flesh and Blood* wanted to hide behind a pseudonym. It gave an idea of the plot, and it mentioned Timworth and Finwood by name. Said they must be laughing all the way to the bank."

"Well, I didn't see it."

"Suppose you had," Dougal said. "Suppose you'd left the typescript or your word-processing discs in Muswell Hill, along with all the other things you left. Maybe you wrote the book when you were pregnant, and maybe Oz told you it was total crap and you put it away in a drawer. And then, when you saw that piece in the *Sunday Times,* you realized that Oz must have dug it out and thought he could use it to raise a quick buck from Gasset and Lode. He thought the book would fail, everyone did, that you'd never hear about it because no one would read it. Of course he couldn't tell Timworth who wrote it, because Timworth's in love with you. So he had to pass it off as his own. And then the unthinkable happened: the book was a success. And that's why you asked him to Halcombe, and that's why he came. You wanted at least a share of the profits. What happened then?"

"Nothing happened. I hadn't even heard of that bloody book."

"I think Oz told you to get lost. He told you that you could never prove you wrote the book. And when you threatened to tell the world about it, he laughed in your face. What was there to tell? Okay, he might just possibly have lost his job—assuming you could have proved that he and Timworth conspired to defraud Gasset and Lode. But that wouldn't have been easy because everyone knew that you and Oz hated the sight of each other. He'd have said you'd made the whole thing up out of spite. Your word against his. And it was even less likely that you could have proved you were McQuarm. In financial terms, that was the important thing, that was where the money was. I wonder what he intended to do. Carry on as McQuarm himself?"

"I don't know why I'm listening to all this," Lesley said coldly.

"You're listening because you want to know how much I can prove. And I'm talking because I'd like to know if there's anything I've got wrong. One of the reasons you went to Muswell Hill after

178   ANDREW TAYLOR

the funeral was to collect anything that tied Finwood to McQuarm. You didn't just take the bank statements and the Samuel Palmer. You took the computer discs as well."

"How do you know?"

"That doesn't matter. But it is something I could testify to in court."

"Were you there?"

Dougal shrugged. "I can also testify to the bonfire you had. You remember? Yesterday morning? Funny time to have one—you'd just got back from London. And Olivia said you'd been to the rubbish dump."

He slowed for a roundabout. They turned on to the dual carriageway that led to the motorway. Dougal noticed absently that the car seemed to be driving itself. He hadn't eaten since breakfast. You couldn't hope to subsist indefinitely on a diet of excitement, worry and cigarettes.

"Even if I were McQuarm," Lesley said suddenly, "so what? Why are you going on about it?"

"Because it supplies the motive."

"Oz's death was an accident."

"If you're right about that, it was a remarkably fortunate one. But it's not your husband's death I mean. It's your brother's."

Celia had never had much time for Simon, the aging hippy who lived in the flat above William's. He claimed to make his living by importing organically-grown herbs but his main occupation was smoking dope. She suspected him of being a bad influence on William.

When she arrived, however, Simon confounded her with kindness. It was nearly six-thirty but William's windows were still in darkness. Simon ran downstairs with the key and insisted on carrying Eleanor, asleep in her reclining car seat, from the Volvo up to William's flat. Later, he went out in the rain to buy the disposable nappies that Celia had forgotten to bring with her. Best of all he didn't ask questions.

"Anything you want," he said as he left, "just ask."

The flat was as familiar to Celia as her own home. She had lived here for a few weeks; and it was even possible that Eleanor had been conceived in the bedroom. Nevertheless she felt like a prying stranger as she peeped into the living room at the front, the small bedroom at the back, the kitchen, which was the size of a shoebox, and the thin little bathroom.

The place was sparsely furnished and agreeably clean. There were, thank God, no surprises, apart from the photographs on the chest of drawers in the bedroom. One was a shot of Eleanor, which Celia had given him last month; William had gone to the trouble of having an enlargement made and buying a frame. The other was an old black and white one of herself, looking young and alarmingly earnest. The fact that it was on display gave her a reassurance that she wasn't sure she wanted.

At the back of Celia's mind, well buried under a mound of common sense, was the possibility that someone else might occasionally share this flat. Well, why not? She could hardly expect William to remain unnaturally celibate for the rest of his life. Perhaps on such occasions he had the decency to put her photograph away.

She drew the curtains, lit the gasfire and put the kettle on. While she waited for the water to boil, she ran her eyes along the books that filled one wall of the living room. A paperback copy of *The Single Father* nestled beside a light blue hardback called *The Scientific Investigation of Crime*. It occurred to her that, if you knew the dates they'd been bought, books alone would provide you with a basis for their owner's biography.

The kettle boiled. Eleanor was still asleep, snoring lightly. Celia made tea. She sat in William's chair by William's fire and tried to concentrate on *The Single Father*. In the background traffic rumbled on Kilburn High Road, the fire hissed and the rain pattered against the window. Celia listened to the sound of Eleanor's breathing and the soft thudding of her own heart.

This time the silence lasted for longer. Dougal thought it had become a sort of contest, a pointless trial of strength to determine which of them had more need to talk.

The wipers swished across the windscreen. The remaining natural light drained out of the sky, driven away by the red of tail and brake lights, the flashing orange of indicators and the relentless white glare of headlights. They negotiated a string of roundabouts and at last ran down the access road to the motorway. Dougal resisted the temptation to make the car go as fast as it could. What was the use? No one was pursuing him; there was no one to drive to.

Lesley, speaking more loudly than before to be heard above the roar of the engine, was the first to give way: "Do you live by yourself?" she said unexpectedly.

"Yes."

"Where?"

"I've got a flat in Kilburn. Why?"

"I thought you might. You come across as a loner. I know you've got a child but that doesn't necessarily mean anything, does it? You're not gay, are you?"

"No. Did you really think I might be?"

There was another, much shorter silence, and then without warning she reverted to the previous subject.

"Ross either had an accident," she said firmly, as though repeating a lesson to a recalcitrant child, "or someone killed him because they thought he was Oz. Anyone can see that."

"I know," Dougal said. "And obviously that lets out you and your mother. You knew who he was. Ross was doing you both a favour by being there. In any case, you both had alibis of a sort: you were with Timworth and your mother was babysitting."

"Well, then," she said. "I'm glad we can agree on that. How does me being McQuarm, which I'm not of course, give you the motive for his death?"

"Ross needed money very badly. I think he found the McQuarm author file from Gasset and Lode when he went through Oz's things. If nothing else, the file must have confirmed that *Empire of Flesh and Blood* had already made a small fortune."

"It's possible, I suppose. But it wouldn't have told him who McQuarm was."

"He didn't have to be told," Dougal said, "because he already knew. There's a copy of the book in the back of the car. I was looking at it this morning. You remember the bit near the beginning when the mother wants to expand her empire of vice and she needs some working capital? She goes in for a spot of gold-smuggling. The author went in for a lot of detail about that. It seemed unusually authentic. Did you ever meet a little Italian called Julio?"

"I'm happy to say that I don't know any little Italians at all," Lesley said.

"He knows you. I talked to him at lunchtime. He remembers having dinner with you once. It was years ago, before the twins were born. He thought you were pregnant. Ross was there with his girlfriend, and Oz, and of course Mrs. Julio. Julio remembers you asking about how the price of gold was fixed, and how people imported it and so on. Ross asked you why you wanted to know, and you said it might come in useful for a book you were writing, a novel. That's why Julio remembered, you see. For him, writing a book is something special. He even remembered what the title was going to be."

"He must have been lying."

"Don't be silly. There's a service station coming up. Shouldn't you phone your mother?"

Celia was glad when Eleanor woke up. It was good to have something to do, and even better to have company.

Eleanor needed changing and feeding. There were several changes of clothes in the bag that Celia had brought from Kew. After Eleanor had sucked her fill, she and Celia crawled across William's carpet; Eleanor pulled his books from the lowest shelf and brought up some of her supper on the hearthrug. Then Celia bathed her. Eleanor chuckled at the unfamiliarity of her surroundings and produced a new vowel sound to mark the occasion.

Afterwards she fell asleep at the breast. Celia wondered if now was the time to scribble a note of apology, get in the car and drive home. But Valerie might still be there. Anyway, why bother? She felt comfortable, as if the shared responsibility of Eleanor gave her a right to be here; the room was warm; there was food in the fridge; and she still wanted to see William.

She wrapped Eleanor in William's duvet and laid her on the bedroom floor.

While Lesley phoned her mother, Dougal waited in the car. He smoked another cigarette and wondered if he'd prefer her not to come back. A moment later, he watched her running towards him, her hair sparkling with raindrops and her face as bleak as a statue's.

"Come on," she said, "let's go."

Her voice was low and urgent, as though the purpose of the journey were an appointment she couldn't afford to miss. Dougal drove on, keeping just within the speed limit. Lesley was so still and silent that at one point he thought she might be dozing.

She stirred as they passed the last exit to Reading. Soon they were only a few miles from the outskirts of London.

"It really was a shock," she said. "There it was in the paper, in black and white: *Empire of Flesh and Blood* by A. J. McQuarm. All he'd done was invent a pseudonym. He was so bloody confident that he didn't even bother to change the title. And when I saw the money the book was earning, I knew that Oz had told me a load of lies about how poor he was. I phoned him up at work during the week, and he said he'd come down and discuss it."

Dougal's hands relaxed on the wheel. She had let down the first of her defences. He said, "Did you think Timworth knew?"

"That I'd written it? At the time I wasn't sure. Not entirely. I thought not. I didn't think he could have hidden it from me. I didn't think he'd have wanted to. Anyway, when Oz came down, I said, 'Right, I want my cut.' Not for me, I swear, or not very much. It was for Olivia. She *needs* it. Have you any idea what a little money can do for an intelligent child? Or what poverty means if you've got kids? You've got a daughter. Think about it, William. What would you have done in my place?"

It was the first time she had called him William.

"I'd have wanted a share in the profits," he said. "But that's beside the point. What did Oz say?"

"Oz said I could go and screw myself, except he didn't put it quite so nicely. He said the book was his, that now McQuarm was established he'd write a whole string of books under the same name and they'd all make the same kind of money. He said he didn't need anyone's good opinion—mine, Olivia's, Ed's or Gasset and Lode's. He was going to be rich, and that was all that counted."

"And then he fell out of a window and you were rich instead."

"Don't say that."

"The trouble was," Dougal went on, "Ross realized what a little goldmine he'd stumbled on. He'd assumed that Oz was just a struggling publisher, and that all he could reasonably hope for was your mother's brooch on account and maybe a few thousand later from you. But when he saw that file, when he realized the sort of money that was involved, everything changed."

"Look, I admit all that," Lesley said. "It's true that Ross was going to blackmail me. And he would have done, too. Neither of us used the word 'blackmail,' of course, but that's what it amounted to. But I didn't kill him. You know I didn't. I was with Ed."

"What were you doing?"

"Just driving around. I was in a hell of a state—restless, I had to be moving. Ed was good to me."

"A prosecuting counsel could make mincemeat of that alibi. Neither of you seems to know where you went. The McQuarm business gave both of you a motive to kill Ross. And he's—well, emotionally involved with you. I suppose you plan to marry him, just to make quite sure."

"Are you saying we made it up?"

"Of course you bloody did," Dougal snapped. "I went through Timworth's accounts this morning. He files his credit-card slips and ticks them off against the monthly statements. That night he went to the theatre, the Haymarket, and he paid by Barclaycard. So stop trying to drag him into this."

She sniffed twice.

"There's a box of tissues on the back seat," Dougal said.

"I *was* just driving around," Lesley said shakily. "But afterwards, when Ross's body turned up, I thought people might think that was suspicious. So I explained it all to Ed, and asked him to give me an alibi."

"You were driving, all right. You were driving to Sheba's Tump in your mother's car. You knew that Ross was going to phone Halcombe. You knew the geography. And when you got there, you realized that Ross must have walked up to the pub. That was a stroke of luck for you. Or was it? Perhaps you knew he would, perhaps it was all part of the plan to make it seem as though Ross was just a normal visitor, a townee who couldn't wait to strut around in his Wellington boots."

"You can't prove a thing," Lesley said. "You're raving. Maybe it's an occupational hazard."

"Ross must have taken some of his own belongings to the cottage. He'd have needed them, wouldn't he? His passport, for instance. His own clothes. But everything at Sheba's Tump belonged to Oz. What did you do with them? Burn them on your bonfire? Cart them down to the council dump?"

"The killer might have found them, realized he'd got the wrong man and—"

"You think that's likely?" Dougal interrupted. "Anyway, it doesn't matter. The real clincher is the boots."

Gradually unease turned to worry. It was already seven o'clock, and it felt much later. Celia forced herself to eat a bowl of muesli. She kicked off her shoes and curled up in the chair. If only she could sleep.

Suppose something had happened to William. He had always been one of those drivers who give the impression that the cars they drive are like half-wild horses: liable at any moment to throw their riders and gallop off in the wrong direction. Admittedly his driving seemed to have improved. But he might have relapsed into incompetence.

She stood up and wandered round the flat. Into the bedroom to check that Eleanor was still asleep. Into the kitchen to wash up her bowl. She picked up the phone and dialled her own number. It rang on and on. Did that mean Valerie's boyfriend had collected her? If so, Celia no longer had an excuse to stay here.

What did you do if you were afraid that someone might have had an accident? Ring the police? Ring every hospital in London and, if that failed, in the whole of southern England? He could be anywhere. She didn't even know the Sierra's registration number.

"Don't die," Celia said aloud. "We need you."

"Olivia's got her name in her boots," Dougal said. "The first time I met you, she said that Ross's boots had his name in them, that's what gave her the idea. So they must have been kicking around the house. Probably in the porch along with the others. But they're not there now, are they? Your mother told us that Oz's shoes were a bit small for Ross: they pinched. So Ross took his own boots to Sheba's Tump. Black boots, Lesley. Were you listening behind the door tonight when I phoned Mrs. Angram? She noticed the boots because of the mud. Black boots, she said. But when I found Ross, he was wearing green ones."

"It means nothing. He might have—"

"You can't wriggle out of it. Only you and your mother knew that Ross was wearing his own boots, and that they had his name in them. No one else. I can't imagine your mother killing Ross, can you? Besides, you'd left her minding the baby."

"I hate you."

Dougal indicated left. "You were a fool, you know. You ran incredible risks all along. And you shouldn't have touched the boots. You could have said that Oz had borrowed them. But no. You tried to be clever."

The Sierra slid down the ramp from the raised section of the motorway. Ahead lay Chiswick roundabout, from which four choices radiated like spokes from a wheel: home to Kilburn, straight on to Earl's Court, down to Kew where Celia would not be glad to see him or back in the direction they had come from. He moved into the lefthand lane.

"Where are we going?" Lesley said, her voice high with panic. "I thought you were taking me to Ed's."

"I'm going home. I'll drop you at a tube station."

"Take me with you. I want to explain."

"Really? There's nothing left to explain. You killed two people and told yourself that you had to do it, for Olivia's sake. You killed for love. Olivia justifies anything, doesn't she? If it had been just Oz who died, I might almost agree with you, because the whole thing happened on the spur of the moment. But not Ross. He was different."

"Let me come home with you, William."

Suddenly Dougal was angry. Without indicating, he pulled over to the kerb and switched off the engine. The car behind braked, swerved and hooted angrily. Lesley cowered away from him, as though he were the killer.

"And what would you do if I said yes?" he asked. "I know: you'd try to argue. You'd point out how many people would be hurt if the truth came out. Innocent people like Olivia. If that argument failed, maybe you'd switch on the tears, offer to seduce me. And if that failed too, perhaps you'd lose your head and try to kill me."

Something glittered on her lap: the reflection of a streetlamp on a few inches of stainless steel. Her breathing was shallow. Dougal felt weary. Her stupidity disgusted him. The law of diminishing returns applied even to murder. He was mildly astonished by his own calmness, by the absence of fear. *Don't I want to live?*

"Put it away," he said. "Do you think I'd be here if no one knew what I was doing? I left my notes on the case at the office. You'd only make matters worse for yourself."

The plastic raincoat rustled. The blade disappeared.

"What will you do?" she said.

"I'll make a formal report in the usual way. I'll talk to James Hanbury. I shall recommend that we hand over what information we've got to the police."

"You haven't got a case that would stand up in court. And your boss won't be pleased. This won't do much for your firm's reputation."

"That's not for me to say."

"You just do what you're told, eh?"

"I'm trying to do what I think is best."

"Who for?" she cried. "This way no one wins."

He said nothing. The only answer he had would make no sense to her: *best for Celia, best for Eleanor.*

A police car drew up behind them. An officer got out and strolled towards them, fumbling in his pocket for a notebook. Dougal rolled down his window and wondered what he had done with his driving licence. History had a habit of repeating itself.

"You do know you're not meant to park here, sir?"

"Sorry," Dougal said. "I just stopped to let my passenger get out."

Celia didn't move when she heard William's key in the door. She guessed he would have seen the Volvo outside. Relief that he'd come warred with irritation that he'd taken so long about it. And the need for explanations paralysed her.

Leaving the front door open, he almost ran into the living room. His face was white, there were hollows under the cheekbones and his eyes looked huge and very blue.

"Is it Eleanor?" he said. "Where is she?"

"Nothing's wrong—she's asleep." Celia pointed at the bedroom door, which was ajar. "Go and look."

She followed him. The bedside lamp, which she'd shaded with a brown towel and put on the floor, filled the room with a soft, golden light. William, his shoulders shaking, was standing over Eleanor. She was still lying on her stomach, well-covered by the duvet. All you could see of her was the short, untidy hair that glinted in the lamplight, and the tip of a pink ear.

Celia slipped her arm through William's.

"It's all right," she whispered. "It's all right."

ABOUT THE AUTHOR

Andrew Taylor went to school in East Anglia and to university in Cambridge. He has traveled widely, and worked for a time as a librarian in London, but gave up his work to concentrate on his writing. He has published a number of successful books, including the much-praised *The Second Midnight* and *Blacklist.* He lives in Gloucestershire, England, near the Forest of Dean, with his wife Caroline and their children. *Blood Relation* is his Crime Club debut.